Pra

"A chilling and dark work that   r of
Suspen

"Volk's book brilliantly and movingly g...   o
the ambiguous depths and tragic dimensions of the films, and ..   , to
Hitchcock his humanity, the wounded and confused pain and compassion at
the heart of his work" **Jez Winship, Sparks in Electric Jelly**

"In *Leytonstone,* author Stephen Volk manages to take a familiar moment in
cinema lore and, in a brilliant mix of scholarly research and a vivid, wicked
imagination to a dark extreme, creating a one-of-a-kind tale of terror and
suspense. Volk possesses a questing mind and an expansive heart and vividly
paints dark and light sides of the human equation like few others" **Mick
Garris, producer of *Masters of Horror* and *Fear Itself***

"An incredible piece of writing" **Dark Musings**

"Another triumph... There's much to admire here: the skilfully drawn setting,
the vibrantly drawn secondary characters, the surprisingly moving coda...
Volk's precise and supple prose is the perfect vehicle for his tale. Whether
you view *Leytonstone* as horror, historical fiction or character driven literature
is irrelevant. It's quite simply one of the first must reads of 2015" **James
Everington, This Is Horror**

"A weighty tale, sometimes innocent and charming, often darker and grittier,
but never once putting a foot wrong. Superbly written, atmospheric and tense,
this is perfectly structured and never less than gripping" **Mark West, Strange
Tales**

"*Leytonstone* is intensely vivid, handled with sensitivity and poise, and every bit
as impeccably crafted as *Whitstable* was. A thoroughly compelling and elegant
tale" **Dread Central**

"Not only will you find lightning has struck twice, you're now eagerly awaiting
when it will strike next. Stephen Volk is a master storyteller. And what
stories!" **Johnny Mains, editor of *Best British Horror***

LEYTONSTONE

Stephen Volk

Spectral
Visions

spectralpress.wordpress.com

A SPECTRAL PRESS PUBLICATION

PAPERBACK ISBN: 978-0-9932707-2-7

First Paperback edition, June 2015
Printed by Lightning Source, Milton Keynes.
Editor/publisher Simon Marshall-Jones
Layout by johnoakeydesign.co.uk

Cover art by Ben Baldwin © 2015
Spectral Press, 13 Montgomery Crescent, Bolbeck Park, Milton Keynes
Website: *spectralpress.wordpress.com*

CONTENTS

Some people think a film should be a slice of life.
I think it should be a slice of cake.

Alfred Hitchcock

"Desirée... Maxine..."

Pigeons nod at crumbs on a pavement.

"Burly Rose... Royal Kidney..."

Water empties over the flagstones. The winged pests scatter with a grey fluttering.

"Kennebec... Avalanche..."

Dark legs stride in mirror-black shoes. A man scrubs the pavement with the stiffest of brooms.

"Belle de Fontenay... Pentland Javelin..."

Indoors, a small framed picture sits like a window on the Byzantine Lincrusta wallpaper. Francis of Assisi, eyes turned piously upwards, arms outstretched like Christ on the cross, birds perched along them, treating them like branches, and aloft, circling his head and halo.

"Sharp's Express... British Queen..."

In the greengrocer's at five hundred and seventeen The High Road it is evening, but this room behind the shop is dark even at noon. The fruit and veg are out front to catch the sun, but the spuds, like the family, are kept at the back, in the gloom for safe keeping.

"Northern Star..."

The boy sits with elbows up on a plain wooden table, frowning with deepest concentration, hands cupped round his eyes.

"Eightyfold..."

Fred is a chubby little dumpling with a cockscomb of hair on top. (Born 1899—last knockings of the old century, when Victoria was still on the throne—making him just under seven now.)

"Evergood..."

A woman's hand removes the potato from the table-cloth in front of him, replacing it in a flourish with another.

"Up To Date…"

Another.

"King Edward…"

Another—the last, and it's done.

"Red Duke of York…"

She shows him her empty palms. The silent, regal mime of applause that accompanies a miniscule tilt of the head is praise enough to make his cheeks burn. Sometimes it takes a lot to make his mother smile, he knows, but when she does it's like getting a gold medal from the Queen. A V.C. for gallantry. And she *is* the Queen. In this house, anyway. Prim and proper and elegant—so much more elegant than any of his schoolmates' mothers. A different class entirely. And dresses— oh, immaculately. Never seen outside without her white cotton gloves. Spotless. What are the others? Loud-mouthed fishwives, most of them, with brown baggy stockings and bruises where they've been on their knees all day.

"Onions!" he cries. "Test me on the onions now! Please, Mother! I know them all!"

"Back home they say onions are a great cure for The Baldness," she singsongs in her Irish brogue. "Rub the scalp with a spoonful of onion sap, it'd put hair on a duck's egg!"

Fred chuckles, but at the sound of the latch the moment between them is lost, and so is the chortle in his throat.

His father comes in, taking off the flat cap which confers him a degree of status to those he employs, and hangs it on a peg. Unties the knot of his tan apron at the small of his back and dips his fingers in the font, quickly genuflecting to Our Lady before hanging up the apron on the hook behind the door.

"The sailor home from the sea," Fred's mother says, as if some joke is being shared between her and her son. Fred twitches a smile, but just as swiftly it is gone and he lowers his eyes.

His father washes the earth off his hands under the tap at the Belfast sink. Water runs black down the plug hole. The soap is an unforgiving brick. A disinfectant smell bites at the air. There is no mirror, but while his face is still wet he flattens his moustache and eyebrows with several strokes of a forefinger and thumb.

"Father, I've been learning how to—"

"Is he ready?"

The stiff tap turns off with a harsh twist leaving a stain of grime where the man's thumbs went. He dries his hands briskly in a tea towel.

"Now, Bill," his wife says. "Just a little longer…"

"No." For once he gives her no quarter. He is adamant. "If it's to be done, let's have it done."

"Name o' God, let him have his tea first."

"Name o' God nothing." He returns the tea towel to its nail and rolls down his sleeves, folding over his cuffs and prodding in the links which he keeps next to his shaving paraphernalia on the shelf. "Fred, put your coat on, son."

Fred's mother rises and lifts the small tweed jacket from the back of Fred's chair and the child puts it on. It matches his shorts exactly. It's a suit like that of a grown man. She crouches in front of him, buttons it up, tucks his shirt tail in at the back, adjusts the knot of his little tie. Fred notices her smile is still there, yes—but it is not the same smile as was there before.

"Where are we going?"

"You're going with your father."

She wraps a woolly scarf around his neck. Knots it. *There*.

"Don't mollycoddle him, Em. Leave him."

His father takes a black jacket from its hanger, flicks off dust with his fingers and slips his arms into the sleeves. He takes a different hat—a black bowler this time—from the peg next to the flat cap.

"Come here," says Fred's mother to her child. She gives him a hug—a swift hug, but a tight one, then a kiss on the cheek so hard it almost hurts. She rubs the red stain from her lips off with a licked thumb. Then kisses him a second time, even harder. He tries not to wince. "I'm going to make a great big steak and kidney pie. That's your favourite—a nice big steak and kidney pie, isn't it?"

Fred nods enthusiastically then turns at the sound of a cough.

His father cocks his head for Fred to follow him. Which the boy does, smiling and obedient as ever and smiling because his mother is smiling, after all.

They walk through the shop, the boy behind the man, smelling the sweetness of carrots and parsnips and the cloying heaviness of soil and sacks and straw and the boy does not see his mother sit back at the table, her knees suddenly weak.

When she hears the front door open and close, the shop bell tinkle, she clutches her rosary beads, closes her eyes tightly and for several minutes thereafter silently prays into her white-knuckled hand to Mary, the mother of her God.

*

As they emerge from the dark interior, his father flexes his hand without looking down. Fred takes it. His own hand is warm and soft but his father's hard and ice-cold from the water. They walk away from the shop side by side. Sheaves of brown paper bags are strung up on butcher's hooks and so are pineapples. Nets full of golden-skinned baby onions sit beside wooden crates full of bananas. The trays of Granny Smiths are being carried inside at the tail-end of the working day. One of the assistants, one he likes, flashes Fred a grin and a wink while a different one with a waistcoat over his apron climbs up a ladder carrying the bucket with which he washed the pavement earlier. At the top of the ladder, whistling "After the Ball is Over" with jaunty vigour, he wipes a wet cloth over the mirrored sign above the windows.

"Where are we going, Father? Are we going to the sweet shop? Are we?"

Pigeons flee in the path of the two pairs of feet. Fred's grey school socks. His father's hobnail boots. Walking near enough in step past a horse and cart. The animal, barely a pony, is shorn half-way up. It has an unattended beard, but it has a horizon. And the name on the cart is the same as the one above the shop.

"Can I have some toffee? A big bit? The sort you break with a hammer? The sort grown-ups get?"

"We'll see."

Fred looks up at his father eagerly.

"Can I?"

"We'll see."

Fred is level with his father's watch chain when he pauses before crossing the road, a dangling 'U' between his waistcoat pocket and his button-hole. His father takes his timepiece out, flips it open and looks at the face then tucks it away again.

*

The sun is sinking and the pigeons go where pigeons go when darkness falls. Fred mentally ticks off the manufacturers' names of cars as they pass. Panhard-Levassor, Humberette. Napier. An omnibus creeps by and he memorizes the number. Next stop, the ice rink. The bus behind it, Walthamstow. He knows the routes by heart. His father has said nothing for fifteen minutes, but then he's a man of few words. That's what his mother calls him sometimes: "Here he is—Man of Few Words." But the remark never made him more conversationally-inclined, possibly the reverse.

They cross the road to a red-brick building. Fred trails the fingers of his free hand along iron railings. Fixed to the bars is a shallow glass box and in the box he sees posters with faces on them. One shows a "heathen"—his mother's word, used ubiquitously—with staring eyes and a beard so stringy it looks as if it was combed with a knife. The one beside it displays a thick-necked lout with a V-shaped scar across his cheek. Next to it a woman with broken teeth, both pathetic and frighteningly aggressive, stares out at him. All three gone in a flash, but he has time to register the word "WANTED" above each of them.

He accompanies his father up a flight of stone steps in through a swing door under a blue lamp.

Inside, his father sits him on a plain wooden bench and Fred watches as he walks to a large desk behind which stands a policeman with a sergeant's triple chevrons on the sleeves of his black uniform. As if in competition, the policeman has an even bigger and darker moustache than his father's—"black as sin" his mother would say—and a razor-sharp centre parting that matches his ramrod-straight back and military bearing. It takes Fred a moment to pin it down, but he reminds him of illustrations in the *Pictorial* of Viscount Kitchener of Khartoum at the Rawalpindi Parade when the Prince and Princess of Wales visited India.

Fred watches as the two men's heads bend closer and they whisper to each other. He cannot hear what they say. He sees only the back of his father's head, the stubble the barber shaves with a razor up to the level of his ears. As he listens, the policeman looks over at Fred with glassy, unblinking eyes.

Fred looks sharply down at his own dangling feet, and is reluctant to look up again. He sees a game of OXO written in ink on his knee during Arithmetic. He sucks his index finger and uses it to rub it off.

He is aware somebody is sitting on the bench directly opposite him because he can see shoes a bit like his mother wears sometimes, but scuffed and worn as if somebody has walked a lot in them. He can smell perfume too, or perhaps slightly stale talcum powder covering up another smell which might be beer. The woman's coat is long and he can see splits in the seams and a worn hem trailing on the floor. Her legs are crossed but they're lumpy and he can see the veins without even trying. She has a large nose for a woman and a cleft in her chin. Her head sways and her eyes struggle to stay open. Her face is white with pink blobs on her cheeks. As Fred stares—he can't help it—he can see the dots of whiskers sticking up through the white pan-stick. And the thick-knuckled hand that lifts a cheap cigarette to her lips has long black hairs on the back of it.

Fred looks down, then over at the desk.

Both his father and the policeman are looking at him, then his father beckons him with a single crooked finger.

Fred walks obediently over.

The policeman finishes what he is writing with a sharp dot.

"This is him, is it?"

He comes round the desk. The handcuffs on his belt with the snake-shaped buckle are level with Fred's face. He extends a big flat of the hand, thumb curled up like a hook. Thrusts it towards Fred.

Fred retreats a step and sways unsteadily, looking up at his father.

His father nods.

Thus reassured, Fred takes the policeman's hand and shakes it, as he's been taught to do. He's been taught manners. He thinks the policeman is being friendly, and he thinks he is being friendly back. But the policeman doesn't let go. He just keeps shaking Fred's hand until Fred thinks it's time he let go of it, please. But the policeman doesn't.

Fred looks at his father but his father doesn't say anything. Perhaps he doesn't know anything is wrong. *Is* anything wrong?

The policeman walks away but to Fred's surprise he still hasn't let go of his hand yet. He is taking his hand with him. He is taking *Fred* with him.

Fred is confused. The policeman leads him towards a corridor of the police station.

Looking back over one shoulder then the other, Fred expects to see that his father is following them. But he isn't.

His father is just standing there. Arms hung straight at his sides. Bowler hat in one hand. Then he places it on his head.

Fred tries to use the soles of his shoes for brakes, to no avail, as he enters a corridor lined with heavy doors.

He tries to prise his fingers out of the policeman's big hand, but it's impossible. The man's grip is like iron—it has to be like iron, for handling criminals. That's obvious. But he isn't handling a criminal. He's handling a *boy*. A boy who is making little squeaky noises now. Who doesn't want to, but can't help it. Who starts to struggle and squirm but the policeman doesn't even look down at him.

Craning over his left shoulder then his right, Fred looks back down the corridor—which smells of wee—but there's no-one there any more, back standing by the big desk, and this draws out his voice, echoing from the tiles.

"Father? *Father?*"

He feels his ear twisted and pulled vertically, hoisting him onto tip-toes. It hurts like the fires of Hell and he has no choice but to follow it, yanked as it is into the dankness and dimness of a tiny room where the smell of wee attacks him like a dog. Just as suddenly his ear is emancipated and he nurses it, red and sore, whereupon almost immediately it is treated to reverberating clang.

Sensing abandonment, he spins round to see that the heavy door has been shut, cutting out what baleful light the corridor afforded, and he is alone. He flattens himself against it. Disembodied keys rattle as they turn in the lock.

"Father! Father!"

The peep-hole shrieks open. The beady eye of the policeman peers in.

With a gasp of fright, the small boy backs away into the room of wee. Of wee-stained underpants. Of fear.

"Now then, now then. I thought you was supposed to be a Well Behaved Little Boy." The voice rasps just as the lock rasped.

Fred goes quiet.

The peep-hole scrapes shut.

He can hear the echoing of the policeman's squeaky boots, the shiny key ring chinking on the man's black hip. He backs up further, until he sits on the creaky bed with its nasty symphony of rusty springs.

He looks at the long black shadows of bars cast on the floor. The big, grim door facing him. The four filthy walls.

"Father! Father! Father! Father!"

Another door slams, more distant, but loud enough—startling him, and he starts to sob from the bottom of his little heart.

*

A soggy dusk has fully established itself as his father wends his way back to The High Road. His hands feel icy and he puts them in his pockets but doesn't look back. He wants to get home but he isn't sure he wants to get home. He reaches the shop. A glow of sorts radiates from an upstairs window, though net and drape. The lads have packed the boxes of produce neatly inside. He expects no less of them, but it gives him some measure of pride.

"'Night, Mr Hitchcock."

"'Night, George."

He goes inside. Locks the shop door as he always does on the dot of six. Turns the sign from "OPEN" to "CLOSED". He looks at his fob watch. Hesitates. Then comes out again and locks the door from the outside.

His local is the Ten Bells. They know him there, but he isn't a soak. Nor is he there for idle chatter. He never is.

He admires the pint of stout in front of him while it settles, black separating from white, and when he is ready but not a moment sooner he downs it in one, long, slow, sure swallow.

The barmaid, cleaning glasses, flesh dimpled on her arms, watches him in some kind of awe. She is blowsy and his wife would call her 'common'. Her bust is more ample than most, and not unpleasant for that, but what warms him more is how sure she is in her skin. His head tilts back as the last of the nectar drains. His neck muscles pulsate. His Adam's apple bobs as he drains the last mouthful. And when he has finished he places down the empty glass as indemonstrably as would seem possible.

The barmaid continues to look at him with a half-set, half-joking smile, full of knowing and forbidden promise. Which is lost on him, or not, as the case may be.

*

Beyond the window a lamp-lighter whistles "My Dear Old Dutch". Fred weeps quietly to himself as a glow from outside illuminates the cell with a dull triptych thrown onto the back of the door. He pulls up a moth-eaten blanket over his cold, bare knees. The blanket has a hole in it. It also smells of something vile. Fred sniffs it and his face is punched by the rank niff of stale urine. Piss. He thinks of the word they use in the playground. *Piss*.

Echoing footsteps approach. He stiffens and sits up.

"Father... Father?"

He wipes his eyes, staring at the cell door.

"I'm not your father," says the policeman. "Do you want to speak to your father?"

"Yes, please."

"Well he's not here, is he?"

Fred's face creases up. He tries not to cry. Tries to be brave.

"Oi, oi! Stop that snivelling! Cor blimey! Take it on the chin. Take it like a *man*, for Gawd's sake!"

"Sorry."

"Sorry what?"

"Sorry, sir."

"That's better."

Fred hears a rasp. Out in the corridor, the policeman has gone to look through a different peep hole. Check on another prisoner. Fred hurries to the door, fearful he will be left alone again.

"Please, sir. Sir? When's he coming back?"

"Who says he's coming back?"

"He—he's got to come back. He's got to take me home. For tea."

"Oh, he has, has he?"

"Yes."

"Why's that?"

"I haven't done anything wrong."

"Haven't you?"

"No."

"What? Never done *anything* wrong? Not *ever*?"

"No."

"Little lamb whose fleece is white as snow, are we? That's what your mother calls you, isn't it?"

"How do you know that?"

"Isn't it?"

"Yes."

The policeman puts his face up close to the heavy door. "Well, how come you're in 'ere, then—eh?"

"I don't know! Tell me. Please! What did I do? What?"

"You thought nobody was watching, but they were. Everybody was watching. *Everybody*."

"No. It wasn't me. I didn't do anything. There's been a mistake!"

"That's what they all say."

"Who?"

"Criminals."

"I'm not a criminal! I'm a little boy!"

The policeman's hoarse, pipe-smoker's laughter rings out. It echoes horribly, like a voice from deep down in a sewer. It goes on and on as he finds it funnier and funnier while Fred slides to the floor and covers his ears.

Presently he hears the footsteps depart with the same regularity as they came. A metal grille slides and bangs into place and gets locked with another of the fan of keys on the policeman's vast key ring. In his blackness, shadow of shadows, his gaoler, the policeman, is gone. Footsteps, keys, more footsteps, fainter—then not even that.

*

His father sits at the dinner table with one point of a diamond-shaped napkin tucked in at his throat. A trio of dry lamb chops sit in front of

21

him, daubed with mint sauce. His mother serves up sliced green beans fresh from the shop onto his plate. She then spoons out potatoes from a steaming bowl. One, two, three, four...

"That's enough."

As if he hasn't spoken, though it was more than a whisper, she keeps spooning out more—five, six...

Only slightly raising his voice, he repeats:

"That's enough."

His wife stops, places the bowl down heavily in the centre of the table. She sits down tidily, arranging her skirts and serving herself a more than adequate portion. One chop, two potatoes. (Only eats so much as a bird—a *bird!*)

"Bless us, O Lord," she says, hands clasped as if anxious. "And these Thy gifts which we are about to receive from Thy bounty through Christ our Lord, Amen."

She passes the salt to her husband with a smile he cannot fail to notice, a need in her to indicate to him he should now eat and take pleasure in the activity. Because he would never know this of his own account.

*

"A mother was bathin' her baby one night
The youngest of ten, the poor little mite
The mother was fat and the baby was fin
T'was nawt but a skellington wrapped up in skin..."

Fred is sitting on his terrible bed (wee the bed, *piss* the bed) wiping away tears with the heel of his hand as the singing of the nameless drunk in a nearby cell drifts in like a lullaby.

"The mother turned round for the soap from the rack
She weren't gone a minute, but when she got back
Her baby had gone, and in anguish she cried:
'Oh, where is my baby?', and the angels replied..."

Turning his head a fraction as the voice lurches into the chorus, Fred sees five-bar-gate scratchmarks gouged into the wall. Not just one. Dozens of them. All over. *Hieroglyphics*. He knew that word. He knew all about the Ancient Egyptians...

"Your baby has gorn dahn the plug'ole!
Your baby has gorn dahn the drain!
Your baby has gorn dahn the plughole!
You'll nevah see baby ah-gain!"

Days... Days upon days. How many days do they keep people here? The unanswered question makes his lip quiver all the more as he sinks into a ball, pressing his small body into the corner, tucking his knees under his chin, and covering his ears.

"It wasn't me! It wasn't me!"

*

Out at his desk, the policeman stirs his cup of tea. He's trying to read his newspaper, which is spread flat on the desk in front of him.

"Your baby is perfick'ly happy
He won't need no bathin' no more
He's working his way through the sewers..."

"Oi!" yelled the policeman. "Stop that effin' racket!" At which the drunk almost immediately desists. "That's better. Can't 'ear myself ruddy think out 'ere."

Except Fred's endless sobbing does not desist. Far from it.

The policeman sighs, removes his half moon glasses and folds his newspaper. He stands up in his shiny boots and walks to the door to the corridor leading off. His keys jangle once more, in irritation now. Unlocks the grille, slides it back and walks right up to the door to Fred's cell.

"Blimey. What have we got in here, eh? A girl? That's what it sounds like, from out there. A scared little girlie."

Fred is perched, shivering, on his smelly bed, staring through red-rimmed eyes, shoulders heaving gently.

"I'm hungry, sir. I'm starving..."

"You should've thought of that, matey, shouldn't you?... No steak and tiddly pie in 'ere. No plum duff, I can tell you..." The policeman's face is stony, gargoyle-like in semi-shadow. "No Spotted Dick with nice thick custard in 'ere, son. Just bread and water, if you're lucky. If the rats don't get it first, that is."

Fred quickly lifts his feet off the floor.

"No toys ... No books ... No Mum to tuck you in ..."

"Mother'll come. Mother'll come and get me. I know she will..."

"Bit of a Mummy's boy, are we?"

"No."

"Stay at home with your Mummy, instead of playing with the rough boys in the streets, do you?"

"No."

"What *do* you do, then?"

"Lots of things... Play."

"Play? Who with?"

"Friends."

"What 'friends'? A little bird tells me you haven't got any friends."

"I do. Lots."

"Oh. What do you get up to, then? With these 'friends'? Football? Cycling? Arthur-let-ics? Yer, I can see that. You. Very arthur-let-ic."

"I go. I *do* go. And, and... —watch."

Outside the cell, the policeman folds his arms, leans against the wall.

"And what do you do up in your room for hours on end, eh? All on your own?"

"Nothing. *Nothing*. Read books. Puzzles. Maps. That's all."

"Books? What sort of books?"

"All sorts. Stories... And train timetables. I like timetables better than stories, even. Facts, numbers, times." And suddenly—something he's proud of. Something that might impress. "I've travelled on every tram in London!"

"Ah!" The policeman sniggers. "A real trolley-jolly!"

Fred takes the laughter as genuine interest from a like mind, and spouts

24

forth with the gusto of a true aficionado. "Trains, boats, everything! I love it. I've taken the river steamer to Gravesend, all on my own. I've made a chart that's up on my wall at home showing the positions of every British ship afloat. And, and—I chart their courses and check them every day in the newspapers..."

"Trains, boats... Yer... That kind of information would be very valuable if it fell into the wrong hands."

Fred is taken aback. "What? What hands?"

"You think I was born yesterday? You think I don't know what type of person charts shipping lines on his bedroom wall?"

"No." Fred is frightened now.

"... the type of person who watches people? Watches them and observes them all the time...?"

"No."

"I'll tell you what sort of person. A spy. That's what sort of person."

"I'm not a spy."

"Who would suspect? Clever. *Very* clever."

"I'm not a spy! I'm not *anything*!"

"Don't come the innocent with me, Sonny Jim."

"But I *am* innocent!"

"No you're not. You're as guilty as sin. It's written all over you."

"I'm not guilty. Ask Mother."

"Everybody's guilty of something. Even Adam and Eve were guilty of something, weren't they?"

Fred's eyes fall on a graffito of an erect penis and pendulous testicles scrawled on the cell wall. He jerks his face away from it.

"I don't know..."

"What?"

"I don't know."

"I can't hear you."

"I DON'T KNOW!"

In a quiet tone, feigning both surprise and disappointment, the policeman says, "You don't know very much, do you?"

Fred hears a woman's giggling outside. A passer-by. A lady will help. A lady will understand.

He runs towards the window and jumps up from the mattress to try and catch hold of the bars. He can, just about, but his head doesn't come up high enough to see out. It's impossible. He wishes he had the breath to call out for help. His feet dangle and his hands aren't strong to hold his weight because he is fat. He drops back, onto his knees, on the bed, panting. Facing the grim, blank wall as the woman walks away, staggering from pavement to gutter and back again.

"See, there's such a thing as crime and punishment," says the policeman's voice, soft yet booming, as if from inside a drum. "Even in the Garden of Eden. Crime. Punishment."

"Punishment for what?"

"For being bad. See, you commit a crime, you don't just let your mother and father down, who brought you into this world, you let God down. And you know what happens when you let God down?"

Fred is too scared to answer. The voice coils like a serpent, slippery and encircling the brickwork.

"You go down. Down, down, *down*… You know what I mean by 'down'?"

"Yes."

"That's where you are now. Down. Down in the dark. With the nasty people. The slugs and snails who don't wash behind their ears."

"I wash behind my ears. All the time. Sometimes Mother says you can grow potatoes there, but she's joking. It's a joke."

"Yer, well. There are no jokes in here, I can tell you. I don't hear anybody laughing, do you? Do you?"

"No."

A mischievous expression adorns the policeman's face. He opens the peep hole to Fred's cell and puts his hairy, puckered mouth to it. It has the anatomy of a wound or other aperture.

"You know who's in the next cell?" he intones with mountainous relish. "Jack the Ripper."

Fred stiffens, terrified. Curls up tight, knees under his chin.

"You know who Jack the Ripper is, I take it?... How many women did he top, eh? And just round the corner from 'ere? Whitechapel. How d'you get to Whitechapel from here on the tram? Eh?"

Fred is struck mute.

"Never caught him, did they? No. So you'd better pipe down, or he'll have your giblets for garters, like he did them tarts." The peep hole closes. Then it opens again, an afterthought. The pink mouth is back. The wet wound, growling. "You know what a tart is, Fred boy?"

"Yes."

"What?"

"It's a little piece of pastry with some jam in the middle."

The policeman laughs horribly—even more horribly than before, if that is possible.

"That's right. A little piece of pastry with some jam in the middle. That's what Jack says—don't you, Jack? Jack's having a little chuckle at that, old Jack is."

Sure enough, Fred can hear cackling—*mad* cackling—but he doesn't know if it's Jack like the policeman says or it's the drunk and he doesn't want to find out. He hugs his horrid piss-blanket to his chest.

"Maybe if you ask nicely he'll tuck you in at night, instead of your dear old Mum. That's who we've got in 'ere, see. Murderers who cut you up in tiny pieces. Thieves who steal your money. Spies who watch you when they shouldn't ought to..."

Fred bites into the blanket, wanting to shut out the words, the ideas, the terrors—but he can't.

"People who have dirty thoughts. 'Cause dirty thoughts don't wash away with soap and water, do they, eh?"

Fred shakes his head, great lurching sobs breaking out of his chest now, his chubby cheeks shining from hours of tears.

"Because this is Hell, Fred. That's what it is. Prison is a little taster of Hell, for people who see too much or say too little, people who haven't got any friends, or whose eyes are too big for their bellies... that's what prison is."

And Fred wants it to stop now. He can't bear it any more. It's overwhelming him uncontrollably. Stifling him. Suffocating him. And all he can do is shudder and rock and mumble like a prayer:

"Mother'll come. Mother'll come and explain. Mother'll come and get me. I *know* she will..."

"Will she?"

"Yes. She loves me."

"Does she? Oh, I don't think so. Not any more. Not after this. Not after what her darling boy's gone and done this time."

"Don't. Don't tell her. *Please!*"

"Nothing can save you now... Not your Dad, not your Mum. Not God. Nobody."

"I want to go home. Please. *Please*. Please let me go home..."

"This *is* your 'ome. You'd better get used to it, Freddie boy. This is your 'ome now. For the rest of your born days."

By this point young Fred is beyond mere weeping. Every ounce of him is weaker than jelly. He feels drained through a sieve. Diminished. The rind scraped off him, the juice running out.

The policeman, having carried out his self-given duty with not a little pleasure, turns and walks away, shooting the cuffs of his dark uniform. Army boots polished to oblivion clinking against the flag stones as their music recedes.

Fred can hardly breathe. He thinks he might choke. His throat is swollen from weeping and the salty saliva builds in his mouth because swallowing is too painful now. But the emptiness and loneliness is more painful still. And worst of all, he doesn't understand. Everything— *everything*—is a mystery...

"Nighty-night!"

The policeman switches off the corridor light with the brisk click of a chain pull. The grille shuts heavily and finally, with a clang that reverberates though the small boy's skull.

Easing back onto his perch, the policeman shakes his newspaper to its full swan-wing breadth and returns to the sports results. His tin mug of tea is stone cold and so is the pot.

"By the way, tuck them toes in," he calls out with some measure of glee, as a footnote. "The rats get a bit peckish in the wee small hours."

*

His father habitually sleeps as soon as his head hits the pillow, but tonight, while his body is weary, his mind is active. Perhaps it was the stout. His bladder feels full, but he fights the need to empty it and tries again to drift off. His eyes open in the dark and he turns round in the bed from one shoulder to the other, noticing that the space beside him is empty.

Propped on an elbow, he sees his wife, Emma Jane, wrapped in her dressing gown with a green cardigan loosely draped over her shoulders, sitting at her vanity mirror, face triplicate in the mirrors. She sniffs into a handkerchief as if she doesn't know he is watching. A porcelain martyr gazing at herself with the kind of self-examination bordering on punishment he abhors. He wonders how long she has sat there while he snored, clearly unable to sleep—or so she would have him think. What would she have him think? And to what lengths would she go to have him think it? She amazes him every day. And here, now, wringing the moment for every ounce of tragedy she could muster.

"My baby. My poor baby…"

He droops his head, rubs his eyes and sighs, wondering how long this night will be.

"How can you do that to him?" she asks, not meeting his eyes in the mirror. "How?"

His answer is to turn his back on her.

"Aren't you speaking to me? Why aren't you speaking to me?"

Her husband closes his tired eyes.

"You're a monster," she says with a tremor in her voice. Then it's no more than a breath. "A *monster*."

*

The boy hasn't slept a wink, and yet the dawn creeps up on him. He lies buried under the sticky blanket, where his sniffles can be muffled and he can hide from the accusing walls. His covering has remained cold through the night, and only when he peeks from under it, after hearing the traffic increase in the street outside, does he see the shadows of the bars cast sharply on the back of the door by the morning sunlight.

He blinks and unwinds himself. The huddled shape of him quivers and his stomach rumbles, having missed both tea and supper. He is frozen and pulls up his socks to get warm. He itches, scratches and thinks of insects seen and unseen. Then buries himself back against the wall like a cocoon and tries to sleep—though by now the noise of guttural engines and piping car horns from the street is making it impossible. The sounds go through him and he wonders if being awake forever would be even more horrible than being asleep forever, than being dead. It is the kind of thing you read in the tales of Edgar Allan Poe. That not sleeping sends you mad, and he wonders how long it might be before *he* goes mad. He wants to cry again, but at the sound of footsteps he sits up, hair tousled, on the crummy bed with big, startled, sleep-craving eyes.

A key rattles in the lock.

Someone opens the door with one hand.

Fred holds his breath, hoping it isn't the same policeman, but it is. The creature's silhouette fills the doorway but he sees light beyond.

"All right, Jack the Ripper. Let's be having you."

He doesn't sound the same now, and Fred wonders if he was sleeping and dreaming after all.

After he blinks he sees the policeman is gone and the door is open, leaving the way clear for him to walk out into the corridor, which he does.

The battalion of keys jangling on his hip, the policeman is walking back to his desk. He stops and offers his hand, fingers splayed, without looking back. Fred doesn't take it. Just stops dead too, with a small gasp of fright, then, when the policeman starts moving again, walks four or five paces behind him, upping his pace to hasten through the metal grille before the policeman slides it shut and locks it.

Fred sees his father. Flat cap. Tweed suit. Waistcoat. Starched collar and tie. Sitting on the bench where he himself sat the evening previously.

"Father?"

The man is already in the process of getting to his feet, saying:

"Behaved himself, I hope?"

The policeman sharpens his pencil, turning the lever with a whirr. Grinds the lead to a point. Blows off the shavings.

"I think he's learned his lesson."

His father walks to the desk and puts a box of fruit and veg in front of the policeman, who lifts it off onto the floor beside his stool. Taking an apple from the top, he rubs it over the heart of his black, buttoned uniform taking a single chunk into his mouth which bulges in one cheek as he chews.

The transaction complete, then—and only then—does his father look down at his offspring, still reluctant to meet the boy's bleary, red-rimmed eyes.

"Now you know what happens to naughty little boys," he says.

Fred blinks. Sniffles. Nods.

The man holds out his hand. Fred takes it. His father's grip is firm and tight. A little too tight. Fred rubs his nose with his other hand to stop it running. A silvery trail coats his finger. He doesn't know what to do with it.

"Come on."

Fred looks back over his shoulder at the policeman.

The policeman winks.

Tweaking the ends of his moustache into points, he watches the fat little boy and his father walk out into the morning sunlight. Envying them their humdrum day, he opens the large book under his elbows and writes the date atop of a blank, sullen page, ready for the woes of the populace.

*

Without letting go of his father's hand, Fred looks back over his shoulder at the police station. It shrinks in scale. Around them London is starting to wake. Draymen on a brewery vehicle idle past at the clip-clop pace of the cart-horse. A blind man begs. Coalmen deliver sacks. Their ignorance almost makes the boy feel the night before never happened. Perhaps it didn't. If it did, why is everything so normal? Why isn't the world different? Changed?

He doesn't feel he wants to cry any more, or scream, or shout. He just feels nothing very much. Not even happy. Not even now that he's out and free and has his dad to protect him. He doesn't feel free at all. It's a funny feeling, and one he can't explain.

He walks—not runs, *never* runs indoors—through the criss-cross of busy shop assistants towards Mother, who rises then drops to a crouch to hug him tightly to her bosom. Tight enough to break him.

"My brave, brave boy!"

His father follows, hanging up his cap and wrapping on his work apron.

"Look at the bags under your eyes." She combs her boy's hair with her fingers. "Up the wooden hill for you, young man." Sniffing tears—perhaps she has been chopping onions—she takes him by the hand to the bare wooden stairs leading to the rooms above.

"He's got school to go to," her husband says.

"Don't be ridiculous! Look at the colour of him."

He looks in the mirror, not at his son. "Go and get your uniform on."

The boy obeys, ascending the stairs on his own.

"He can't go to school without something warm inside him." Defiant, she follows.

Below, a figure knots an apron behind his back and goes into the shop to work. Work is what he does best, and what he understands.

*

In the kitchen his mother snips flesh-coloured sausages from a string and drops two into a frying pan. As they sizzle and brown, filling the room with a fatty aroma, she saws a slice of bread into triangles, to fry those too. A rasher of streaky bacon, mushrooms and a bisected tomato (but no eggs, he hates eggs!) are cooked in the same greasy pan, feast enough for a Navvy presented in a mound before a tiny little boy now dressed in his immaculate school uniform. Black jacket, stiff Eton collar and tie, short trousers. Knife in one hand, fork in the other. Starving hungry. Getting stuck in as his mother watches, hands on her hips and happy, though still dabbing at the residue of what he knows were tears. It makes him feel bad, so he eats, because he knows that makes her happy. He even smiles, and for a moment thinks she might burst into tears. Has he done something wrong? He doesn't know, so he just keeps on eating.

"Please may I leave the table?"

His father comes in just as Fred finishes breakfast.

"You may."

Fred brings over his cutlery and crockery to her, like a good boy.

"That's what I like to see—a nice clean plate."

He pulls his satchel strap over one shoulder and puts the school cap emblazoned with the letters 'S.I.' on his head. His mother bends for a kiss on both her cheeks, after which ritual he leaves by the stairs leading down to the back of the shop.

The boy having gone, his father sits in the same chair waiting for a similar cooked breakfast to be put in front of him, if with less grace. Fred's mother immediately turns away and busies herself washing the other dishes.

"He's got to toughen up. Don't you see that? All I want to do is protect him." But the man is talking to his wife's back, and isn't surprised when she doesn't deign to answer.

He stares at the food, cutting and chewing without the delicacy or poise she'd like, as she leaves him to enjoy his meal in the room alone.

*

Has he done something wrong, after all? Was the policeman right? Fred can't help thinking about it as he trails a finger along the bars, the prison bars, no—the iron railings of Saint Ignatius Catholic School for Boys, Stamford Hill. He grips them and looks through at the sight of a flock of young Jesuit priests playing football, black robes tucked in or knotted in bunches between their legs. They attack the ball with intense vigour. Their faces masks of simian concentration, ears protruding from severe haircuts. Shoes fly. Shins crack. Cassocks wheel. Mouths twist. Fists bunch. Arms gesticulate. Perspiration shines. Shaven throats pull raw against white dog collars as veins bulge. Legs blur.

*

In the hermetic gloom of the chapel stands an elderly priest with the wrinkled, desiccated skin of a Yuletide date. At the lectern, Father Aloysius Mullins faces rows of schoolboys as petrified in the pews as the statues that surround them. His wits may be dimmed by age, but he has a faith as resolute as iron. And saddle-bag jowls that quiver and flap as he orates to his unedified congregation of youths and saplings.

"We live in a world replete with the temptations of evil. And the greatest of these temptations is *frivolity!*"

Sitting amongst his peers, Fred silently gazes past the speaker to focus on the large carved statue of a crucified Jesus beyond him.

"By *frivolity* I mean all the things that distract us from our duty to God. By *frivolity* I mean music halls! I mean gramophone recordings! I mean picture palaces! I mean skating rinks! I mean the petty mingling of males and females…"

Christ on the cross hangs frozen in agony from his torments—face distorted, wounds spilling beautifully rendered droplets of blood.

"Be warned! These places deceive you by claiming they are life. They are not life! They are death! The death of your precious moral being!"

Gliding black shadows, a number of seemingly identical younger priests—the football-players—walk the aisles with stiff canes slapping against their legs. Their crow-eyes scan the assembly, eager to pounce on the slightest infraction. The schoolboys, Fred included, sit straight-backed, rigid with fear, terrified of the punishment that could descend on any one of them at the least provocation—or no provocation at all.

The old priest's eyes skulk behind narrow slits shielded by lenses the thickness of ale bottle bottoms.

"If we succumb to them, we succumb to the putrid. We succumb to the beast. By even *contemplating* them, we are giving our names to Satan!"

Fred thinks about Father Mullins' words as the boys later file past the priests, as they always do, to receive the holy wafer. There is a predictability in Communion today that comforts Fred, even though he is afraid. He is always afraid. The fear never goes away at school because it is never *meant* to go away.

"This is the vast peril of your lives. The vast cost that will be paid for abusing the God-given privilege of having *souls!*"

After the *Ave Maria*, Father Malachi administers the goblet of wine. Father Mullins places a wafer on Fred's tongue and makes the sign of the cross. Fred feels something invisible on his tongue. It tastes of nothing and Fred wonders, as he does often, whether it should. Does everybody else taste something, and is it only he who does not?

*

He stands in the rain-wettened playground, alone. This is not unusual. He is often alone. He doesn't mind. He likes his own company. In fact, most of the time he prefers it. He watches the other children and he doesn't think he belongs with them. They aren't like him. That's what his mother says. And often he thinks they might hurt him, and often he is right. When he is on his own he sometimes likes to dream up stories about them. Just think of exciting things that might happen to them, or crimes. Crimes he could solve, cleverly, and be a hero. Or just exciting things like war or jungle stories or adventures with chases and motor cars and danger. Or being trapped. Or something horrible and scary happening.

"Cocky!"

Fred turns. It's Parkhill, beckoning. It's actually a group of three individuals in uniforms identical to his own. The other two are Murphy, red-haired and so Irish-looking it saddens, and O'Connor, less so. Not posh but, like him, lower middle-class Cockney sparrows. If anything a bit threadbare. They go into a conspiratorial huddle, heads down. Fred hurries over to them and joins in.

"There's a hole in the wall of the lavvies, and you can see right through to the girls' next door." Parkhill's face is full of rattish glee. "When they drop their skirts and knickers you can see their fannies and *everything!*"

The boys look at each other with hungry eyes, barely, if at all, understanding why they should take an interest in such things, beyond the fact they are forbidden and if observed, the fires of Hell will rain down upon them for their misdeeds. But that is reason enough, for boys. For Catholic boys in particular. And they run off, and Fred runs with them.

*

The urinals are daubed with the sickly yellow of usage. White tiles echo with the scampering of small, eager shoes. The lads scuttle into one empty, filthy cubicle. The stink—but not the stink—makes Fred hang back with his neat socks and smart jacket. Murphy beckons him excitedly. Fred is thinking about wrongness, and what his mother says, and what the policeman said, but he is thinking also about doing what his friends want him to do.

Parkhill extracts a bolus of newspaper which is plugging up the now-infamous hole. He holds it in the air, trophy-like.

Fred takes a single step closer. He sees the others crowding in, jamming their heads together to get an eye to the aperture. A toilet chain sounds on the far side of the wall and the boys giggle and titter into their hands, then cover their mouths secretively.

"What is it?" Fred asks.

The boys are busy whispering, blushing, poking each other.

"Let me see."

They move aside and Fred sees the peep-hole gouged out of the wall. It looks like a wound. Something vicious, made by a dagger or weapon. He hesitates, nervous now. Not sure at all if this is a good idea.

"Get an eyeful," says Parkhill, sibilant amongst the dirty tiles. "It'll put hairs on your chest." The other boys giggle.

Fred moves between them and kneels on the rim of the toilet seat. Palms against the sticky wall either side, he slowly presses his eye to the hole. Light shines dimly from the other side. His eye lashes flicker. He sees something indistinct.

The policeman's eye stares back at him.

He recoils with a sudden jerk, retreating away quickly, past his friends and outside the cubicle until his back hits the far wall.

His pals look shocked and glances shoot to and fro between them, their eyes then converging on him. The cigarette that Parkhill has in his mouth ready to light up droops.

Fred stares at the small, round hole stiff with horror, mouth wide open and eyelids pulled back, gasping in short little bursts.

"Bloody hell," says Parkhill, snatching the crumpled Woodbine from his lips. "It ain't *that* bad."

*

A hand bell tolls in the jerking motion of Father Boyle's fist as Fred crosses the playground at speed, head hunched over. The priest looks barely older than some of the boys he teaches. Eyes narrowing, he sees Fred shoot a quick look back at the lavatory building. Father Boyle looks over at Father Nolan-Keegan, wordlessly bringing it to his attention. The two priests turn in unison, walk over to where Fred emerged, and go inside. The bell is placed on the ground.

Fred stops in his tracks and turns around. He stares at it. As soon as the two priests are inside he is in no doubt that something bad will result. He chews a thumb nail, then, remembering the reprimands he gets from his mother for doing so, stuffs his hand deep in his pocket. He continues staring at the doors with dread anticipation, red patches burning on his cheeks, islands in his otherwise cold skin. He is positive these are beacons already advertising his complicity in the boys' thoughts about the hole and what they might see but can't do anything to stop it except press his frozen palms to the sides of his face to make them go away.

Though he doesn't have to wait long. It's less than a minute before Father Boyle comes out holding Parkhill by the scruff of the neck and Father Nolan-Keegan follows clouting the other two with the back of his hand.

Fred turns sharply away. He doesn't want to be part of that gang. Not any more. Well, he'll *say* he wasn't, if they ask. He *wasn't*. Not really.

And if they walk past him and he isn't looking at them and they're not looking at him, perhaps the Holy Brothers won't see that he was with them at all. So he'll do that. He'll look the other way. He'll pretend.

Guilty as sin.

He thinks of the policeman's eye again and he thinks of hard boiled eggs. He loathes hard boiled egg sandwiches, sliced with that little egg-slicer in the kitchen—the guillotine type thing he always thought could be the makings of a torture instrument in the wrong hands. In the hands of a murderer, or spy. He didn't like the eye staring at him though. From a hole. He didn't like that one bit. And a little drop of wee (piss) oozes out and wets his underpants. And just then he hears children laughing and he wonders if they know he has just...

He swings around.

A group are looking down at him through railings. Girls from the Convent School next door. Up at a higher level than the boys—both physically and spiritually—they look down on him and his kind like angels in judgement. (When their playtimes coincide, at least.)

Fred blinks, realising that they *don't* know—*can't* know—but are nevertheless giggling into their hands, twisting their knees this way and that under the heavy drapery of their ankle-length skirts, covering their blushing cheeks, turning their backs and exchanging frenetic whispers simply because he is that unknown, unfathomable, mythical creature: a boy. And as soon as he is *looking at them* they are off. Gone. Like a flock of frightened geese taking to the air.

Except for one. A girl with hair the colour of ripe bananas. Of lemons. Of sunlight. Taller than the rest. Slimmer. Straighter. No chest. No *bosom*. None at all. Not like Mother. They don't even look like the same species. She's more like a foal, a colt. And not timid like the others. Not afraid to remain behind for a few moments to have a good look at him. Perhaps as curious about him as he was about her, if that could be possible. What did she find curious or interesting about *him*, for a second, he wonders? Her head is at a tilt, like the picture of Saint Francis of Assisi on the wall at home or one of the Madonnas in the Leonardo da Vinci book in the library. Her face is heart-shaped. Her chin and lips small. Her powder blue school pullover too baggy. It comes down over her wrists and hands. Her fingers are long. Her neck is thin and dove white and unblemished and doesn't quite fit her school uniform collar. Her skin is scrubbed fresh-looking and her hair pulled back in a pale blue bow that matches her eyes. And as he wanders away he can't help asking himself—because they, his *friends*, put the thought there—… what is underneath that dark, voluminous skirt?

*

Outside Father Mullins' study he takes his school cap from a hook, screws it on, and walks down the corridor with his satchel clutched tightly to his chest. The door is on his right. Outside it on a long bench sits O'Connor, weeping and nursing a pulsating red hand. Beside him

Parkhill, who has his arms wrapped tightly around his body and is rocking in mute anticipation of what awaits him.

Cocky... Cocky...

Dreading they might speak to him, and terrified to meet their eyes, Fred carries on past, stiffly, but already beyond the door he can hear the *swish* and stinging *slap* of the ferule as the designated punishment is meted out, slowly but surely. *Swish-slap.* Substance upon flesh. *Swish-slap.* Upon young flesh. *Swish-slap.* Again, child. *Swish-slap.* Again, the punishment. *Swish-slap...* Six times. Always six times. *Six of the best.* Best what? *Swish-slap...*

Trying to block it out, he carries on walking as the door clicks open and his third friend, Murphy, shambles out in a daze nursing a crippled hand against his stomach. The creature-shape of Father Mullins emerges behind him, strap of gutta-percha like a flat ruler hanging from his hand.

"Parkhill."

Without turning, Fred hears Parkhill enter and Father Mullins shut the door. He feels his stomach roll like a yacht in a stormy sea. Quite soon he is too far away to hear the ferule fall, but every few seconds he flinches. He almost considers it his duty to flinch, even though he feels no physical pain himself. It is the least he can do.

*

He arrives home to see his father sawing an ungainly doorstep sandwich on a breadboard. This is not a task to which the man is accustomed, or suited, let alone skilled at, and the boy knows he can only be attempting it of necessity.

"Where's Mother?"

"Having a little lie down. She's had one of her 'turns'."

He knew what that meant all too well. It was strange what could be encompassed in one little word. Especially the way he said it. He wondered whether his father felt sorry for her or cared about her because he didn't show it, not very often. But then Fred knew how she wanted so much, and a lot of the time it was difficult to tell what. One time Fred's father told him she could "change like the wind", and said it like he was tired, or sad, but not angry. Just wishing things could be different, that was all.

*

The cup of tea in its saucer rattles slightly in his hands. The room is dimly lit, curtains drawn, but it is still daylight outside. Nowhere near night-time.

Mother lies in state. Her death bed would be less dramatic. She's a perfectly arranged tableau of listless woe, ready for a painter to commit to oils.

"Oh, bless you, my sweet. Sure who needs sugar when I've got you in the house?" She takes the tea and allows Fred to plump the pillows behind her, then to kiss both her cheeks. "Don't raise your voice today. Your mother has a head on her. She's weak as a bird."

"We could leave it 'til tomorrow."

"You will not." Her limp hand waves him to the foot of her bed, where he stands, ramrod-straight. A ritual that won't be foregone. "Now then. First lesson."

"English."

"And where would you be without your own Mother Tongue?"

"We started Charles Dickens today. *Great Expectations*."

"Ah, Magwich!—terrible man."

"I like him."

"And poor Miss Havisham…"

"We haven't got to her yet."

"In her bridal weeds… If she doesn't break your heart, well, you haven't *got* a heart, that's what I say." She sips her tea. "Next?"

"Geography. We learnt all about rainfall in The Pennines."

"Never a raindrop fell in England that didn't fall tenfold in Ireland. You tell your teacher that. He might learn something."

Fred's mouth tugs a smile.

"Then?"

"Then History. The French Revolution."

"Off with his head! Let them eat cake!"

The boy chuckles. "And in Scripture we did John the Baptist."

"More decapitation!"

Fred nods.

"Who won today? Romans or Carthaginians?"

"We did. Romans."

Fred's mother claps lightly, soundlessly. Fred beams. His cheeks seem to swell.

"And what did you *see* today?"

Fred hesitates. He can't mention the hole. He can't mention the eye. He can't mention Parkhill and his friends, beckoning him to look. He can't mention their punishment. The girls behind the railings tittering behind their hands. What *can* he mention?

"A blue tit and a thrush." He uses his imagination. His imagination is all he's got. "And... and a hearse with four horses, all with black feathers on their heads."

"Plumes!" his mother booms it like a theatrical declamation, puffing her chest, delighted to the point of exclamation by his daily report. Then suddenly remembering her phantom illness, her voice becoming weak and plaintive as that of an injured chaffinch. "To your homework, young man. Make your dear mother proud of you." As pleading and pitiful as if they were the last desperate words she uttered on this sorry earth.

*

A lamentable skin forming on the Bournville cocoa at his elbow, Fred sits at a small table with his homework open in front of him, staring at the curtain covering the window, lost in thought. Snapping out of it, he places blotting paper over the last thing he wrote in his copybook. Rubbing it dry, he puts it in his satchel together with his school text books, which are wrapped in brown paper for protection. He screws the top on a bottle of Blackwood ink and wipes the nib of his pen with an old handkerchief. He buckles the straps of his school bag and hangs it up in an "A" behind the door, eager to get to more serious work undertakings...

His knees land on the bed and he faces a large chart of ships pinned to the wall. He examines it with great intensity. Tugging a newspaper closer, he moves around pins with little flags attached, placing them according to the latest details of the locations of convoys he reads in the small print.

The gaslight breathes on the wall. His bedroom is barely bigger than the awful police cell — but not cold, and not dirty, not for *dirty* people. It's warm, and tidy. The way he likes it. A place for everything and everything in its place. Puzzles and games on the top shelf, books on the bottom. Picture books to the right, novels to the left. In alphabetical order, by author's surname. Just like they should be. Conan Doyle. Stevenson. Swift. And maps almost obscuring the floral wallpaper beneath — the London Underground, together with the Trans-Siberian Railway. He doesn't suppose he'd ever be lost in Siberia, but if he were, he'd know his way around, at least. Knowing maps means you know your way around everywhere. If you know your maps you'll never be afraid.

He takes a sheaf of magazines from a drawer and lies face down on his bed with them in front of him on the pillow.

The top one is an American magazine, *Life* — the cover of which is dominated by an image of the Statue of Liberty. Of course there are statues all over London, but not like this. Not in *colour*. Everything in London is so black and white. He leafs through it, savouring even the shininess of the pages. It feels like success, it feels like happiness, it says excitement, it says glamour. In a way he only flimsily understands, the smiling women in the advertisements say pleasure. Though what kind of pleasure is a mystery. A secret. The kind of secret spies pay money for. And grown-ups kill for. And he devours it. Every word.

Underneath this is *Kine and Lantern weekly*, a cinematic trade magazine. He turns the pages, reading amongst the camera adverts taciturn reviews of the latest releases: *Dick Turpin's Last Ride to York*, *A Slippery Visitor*, and *A Pair of Swindlers*...

He unwraps a mint humbug from his pocket and sucks it as he reads. And as he reads, the pictures play in his head. He can see them happening. The horse's hooves blurring. The flintlock firing. The masked face of the highwayman... Chased by the law for a crime he didn't commit...

He turns onto his back.

The next magazine is *Motor Stories*—described in brazen lettering as *Thrilling Adventure Fiction!* Featuring on its cover a square-jawed driver in a frenetic chase—a lariat thrown from a moving car to catch a man on a bicycle... *Motor Matt: The King of the Wheel!*

The boy's eyes shine. The pursuit. The arrest. The criminal locked up securely behind bars. He looks at the man on the bike. He looks at the square-jawed hero. He looks at the wooden slats of the headboard of his bed. He doesn't like the things that are coming back into his head, but he can't stop them.

He sits up and looks at the back of his hand, and touches it to feel if there are any hairs growing on it. He can feel his heart beating. He bends down to the chest of drawers where his magazine collection is kept. He rummages and digs out one from the bottom of the pile. The one he is looking for. He sits back on the bed, cross-legged, and opens it across his thighs.

It is an edition of *The Illustrated Police News*, its headlines proclaiming THE BERNER ST VICTIM and TWO MORE WHITECHAPEL HORRORS: WHEN WILL THE MURDERER BE CAPTURED? In the central oval a policeman is sounding his whistle. In another box a man is finding FIFTH VICTIM OF WHITECHAPEL FIEND. Next to it a caped policeman's bull's-eye lamp illuminates the MUTILATED BODY IN MITRE SQUARE. He thinks of the woman who wasn't a woman. He feels a prickling sensation on the back of his neck and feels he is being watched. He darts a glance over his shoulder. And he *is* being watched.

On the wall is a painting of Jesus on the coast of Galilee, hands offered, chin upturned, in beatific mode, the blood-red "Sacred Heart" bursting from his chest with golden rods of light. So well painted, his mother says, that "the eyes follow you round the room". And they do. He knows that because he's tried going into every corner, but wherever he does, Jesus is watching.

*

"Hail Mary, full of grace
The Lord is with thee
Blessed art thou among women
And blessed is the Fruit of your womb, Jesus
Holy Mary, Mother of God
Pray for us sinners
Now and at the hour of our death."

In pyjamas, Fred kneels on one side of the bed. His mother kneels on the other. Both have their hands clenched in prayer, and their eyes closed. Then it is time for her not to speak and for Fred to voice an additional bedtime prayer on his own:

"There are four corners on my bed,
There are four angels overhead,
Saint Matthew, Mark, Luke, and John,
God Bless the bed that I lie on."

He opens his eyes and unclasps his hands, but his mother's expression makes it clear he has not quite finished.

"And if I die before I wake," he says,

"I pray to God my soul to take,
And if any evil comes to me,
Blessed Lady waken me."

And they finish, as they always do, by saying in unison: *"Amen."*

"Good boy."

He climbs into the chill, freshly laundered sheets, and she pulls the heavy, stiff blankets up under his chin. Circling the bed, she tucks in the edges tautly under the mattress and comes upon the book at his bedside.

"How is it?"

Treasure Island.

"Scary. Exciting, but scary."

"You and your stories."

His mother leans over and kisses him on the forehead. It's slightly sticky as her lips pull away. He doesn't know whether he likes her doing it or hates it. He doesn't hate *her*—but he doesn't know if it's right for him to like it or if it's babyish. But men like kissing, don't they?

She stands up and turns the hiss of the gas light off. A faint warmish aura spills in from the landing through the half-open door behind her. And he has to ask the question before she's gone.

"Mother?"

"Yes?"

"Is Jack the Ripper still alive?"

Standing at the bedroom door, she laughs lightly at his silliness, poor thing. But it doesn't put his mind to rest.

"Did he dress as a woman? Is that why they never caught him?"

She moves back to the bed and crouches in her gathered skirts. "He ended up in a lunatic asylum. In a room no bigger than this one. For the rest of his days. Don't worry your head about him, now." She strokes his hair three times, then stands and glides back to the door.

"Can I have the light on please?"

She sighs. Walks back and re-lights the gas lamp. Turns it down slightly. Returns to the door. "There."

"Can you please leave the door open? Just a little? Please?" He has the blankets up to his chin, but he lifts his head and shoulders to watch that she does as he asks.

The door slowly closes... — but stops, slightly ajar.

He swallows, his throat moistened by relief.

He sinks back into his big pillow. Into his tightly-wrapped blankets and sheets, as the gas lamp flickers above him. He thinks of the gas poisoning people. Killing them. Murderers using it to put people to sleep. To knock out women. To do what they like to them. And though he wants to sleep, he can't. It's the gas. The gas makes bad things happen. Like the gas lamp outside the police cell window. Every time his eyelids get heavy the sound of the gas makes them snap open again. He doesn't want to sleep because the thing about sleep is, you might not wake up. But if you stay awake and your parents find out you get punished for that, too.

He hears his father's boots ascend the stairs laboriously. The leather squeals and the boards groan.

He holds his breath. He hears his father sit on his bed next door, undo his laces and take off his boots. They fall to the floor. Slam. *Clunk.* He pictures his mother delicately removing the string of pearls from her neck. The bedsprings creak as she gets in beside her husband in the dark.

He hears his father coughing long and hard and a *plop* as he spits into the chamber pot. A few moments of silence later weights shift with the gentle easing of the springs and all is still.

Fred lies motionless. Almost too afraid to breathe. He's not sure why. He doesn't want to be detected. He doesn't want to be found. He is on the run—but he's not sure what he's on the run from, or why.

He turns onto his side. Eyes tightly shut.

The shadows in his room lie replete on the tiny flags on the shipping chart... on his satchel... on the cover of *Robert Louis Stevenson's Treasure Island...*

He pulls up the bed sheets to cover his face, but finds the action has exposed his bare feet at the bottom of the bed. He sits up and hastens to cover them, then lies back quickly and does his best to huddle up, foetus-like under the covers.

He determines to shut his eyes and, much as part of him fights it, lock out everything that is disturbing him, thinking only of sheep, counting sheep, that's it—or telling himself the hot cocoa is calming him like it's supposed to, and his chest isn't turbulent any more.

Little lamb whose fleece is white as snow…

What did he say? Don't think about it. Sleep. Sleep…

And he *tries* to sleep. Just as he did in that cell. That cell that seems a million miles away. That smelly, disgusting cell like one in a dungeon in some story in some fairy tale with an ogre. But he isn't there now. He's safe. He's warm. There is no ogre. No lock and key. He has his mother and father on the other side of the wall. He can even hear them breathing they are so close. He's not locked in. He's not imprisoned. He's not in any danger. He has nothing to worry about at all.

"Wakey wakey!"

His eyes refuse to open.

"Been dreaming, have you?"

The policeman's voice—from the corridor outside.

"Dreaming you were home, safe and sound, I bet…"

Fred's eyes widen as the policeman's laughter echoes like it's coming from that drain, that sewer. From the worst place in the world.

"Well you're not!"

His little tummy churns as he realises first of all that he is not nestled on his nice white mother-puffed pillow: instead his head is resting on his own crooked arm. And the mattress under him is not a mattress but hard wood. And the blankets over him are not his nice thick eiderdown and clean, newly-laundered sheets but the stiff grey, piss-infected blanket of the police station cell.

Which is what he sees around him, now, as his chest caves in. The filthy, scrawled walls. The tiny, iron-barred window with the moonlight beyond.

"You're here. I've got you, matey. I've got you forever!"

The eye.

The eye at the hole, looking in.

Fred sits up—jerks up, gulping air. Gulping enough of it into his lungs to scream—except the scream isn't necessary any more.

The dark, stinking cell is gone.

The room around him is his own bedroom in five hundred and

seventeen The High Street—not the police station at all. He can hardly believe it. That the voice was only in his head. That his imagination— his *fear* – had put it there. And as his body tells him to breathe again, he tries to shake of the reality that was the dream, and the heavy dread that came with it. The knowledge it was a concoction doesn't free him of it. The terror in his bones doesn't listen to reason. Doesn't want to. Can't. Why can't it? Please!

His bare feet hit the icy floor. No time for slippers. He dives to the door, knocking it shut by accident. His small hands wrestle to pull it open and fling it wide.

He rushes into his parents' bedroom, sucking and panting breath as if he has run for miles.

"Can I sleep in here tonight? Can I? Can I? Please! CAN I?"

"*Jee-sus* Mary and Joseph!" His father emerges in curses and groans. "I have to be over to Covent Garden at a sparrow's fart!!"

"Oh, let him be. Let him be!" His mother, wakened by the bang of the door, is already sitting up, if not fully awake. Her arms are outstretched, fingers twiddling, an instinct even before consciousness, and she hugs her son to her night-gowned body.

Simultaneously his father gets out of bed, pulling on his dressing gown from the chair, swirling the tasselled cord and yanking the knot. The man says no more, knowing of old what he has to do and not choosing to make a conversation of it. Not a fan of conversation at the best of times.

*

He pulls the door shut after him, knowing that his son will be taken into his wife's bed and embrace, not for the first time, and too tired to protest about it, the arguments all being well-aired and futile. He cricks his spine, wondering what's the blessed time in the name of God, walking in his darned grey bed-socks to the smaller bedroom down the landing, passing a small, framed photograph of a policeman in full uniform hanging on a nail in the wall.

He shuts the door of Fred's bedroom and hangs up his dressing gown on the hook on the back of it, a large one draped over the smaller one. He sits on the bed, punching the pillow a few times. Gets in. Gets out again and turns off the gas lamp, which gives a low *phut* of annoyance as it extinguishes.

He rolls back on the bed, too small for him by far, tucking his knees up and lying on his side with his back to the door, with no intention of moving a muscle until he has to. And no intention of letting his thoughts—and, Lord knows, there are many—keep him awake. He loses too much sleep over his son as it is.

*

Fred's three friends never mention their punishment and neither does he. He doesn't know if shame compels them to keep it to themselves, or they harbour a resentment that he escaped unscathed. He never asks them if it hurt, though he wants to know, and they don't tell him he's not their friend any more, which he expects. They just behave as though nothing has happened. Which worries him far more than if they did, because he supposes he deserves it. He deserves something.

The end of another school day, and he is walking home with them. Parkhill has something in his cupped hands that Murphy and O'Connor are peeking at. Parkhill looks over at four schoolgirls walking parallel with them on the other side of the road. Fred sees that one of them is the long, lemon-haired girl who stared at him through the Convent School railings.

Her hair is not fastened and falls in a curtain over half her face. Her tie is pulled loose, the way the boys tug open their own the minute they exit the school gates.

"Watch this."

With a jerk of the head, Parkhill leads the other boys across the street to the girls. With a confidence that Fred envies, he stands in front of them, hands in pockets, walking backwards in pace with them.

"Hello, ladies."

"What does S.I. stand for?" One reads the emblem on their school caps.

"Silly idiots," explains the Girl With Yellow Hair.

Her minions titter and snort into their hands. Fred removes his cap as if it is tainted. The fair-haired girl, who seems superior to the others because she is the tallest, parts a way through the boys with her hand like an ice breaker.

"Oi," Parkhill says. "That's not very nice, when we've come all the way over here with a present for you."

The girls stop and turn coldly, almost with pity, and look at them. Curious, but wary. As with everything concerning boys.

"Where is it?" The Girl With Yellow Hair says, affecting only the mildest of interest.

Parkhill shows her the palms of his hands.

"In my jacket pocket. If you want it, you have to take it."

"I don't want it."

"Are you sure about that?"

Parkhill tugs said pocket open with finger and thumb, peering inside tantalisingly.

Fred watches as one of the other girls steps forward but the Girl With Yellow Hair steps in front of her.

"He's talking to me."

"No he isn't," the other girl protests. "Anyway, you said you didn't want it."

"I changed my mind."

The other, dumpy and easily affronted, slumps off in a sulk. "Maria!"

Her friend, black hair in pigtails, flounces off with her. "Silly idiots!"

"I don't want it anyway," the dumpy girl hurls back at them. "—whatever it is."

"Well?" Parkhill says. Two left. "Who's it going to be?"

The skinny, freckle-faced girl is keen, but looks nervous, tugging at her lower lip. The Girl With Yellow Hair waits for her to make a move for it, but when she doesn't, The Girl With Yellow Hair does so herself.

She reaches out to put her hand in Parkhill's pocket—then pauses, staring Parkhill squarely in the eyes. Hoping something might be revealed there, but Parkhill's grin gives nothing away. It's a gamble she will have to take.

Fred watches. Waits.

She looks at her freckle-faced friend, then back at her other two, who are waiting at a considerable distance now. Then, unexpectedly abandoning the last vestige of caution, she plunges her hand deep into Parkhill's pocket. A hesitation, then—

She retracts it with a piercing *SHRIEK*.

Fred jumps in fright, just hearing it.

The Girl With Yellow Hair backs away quickly, mouth wide open in an "O", her chest rising and falling rapidly.

"You horrid, *horrid*—!"

Grinning, Parkhill takes the "present" out of his pocket. A mouse—a wild one caught in the bushes near the playground, tiny and brown—which is now running over one of his hands then the other with its miniscule pink paws and black pearl eyes. Murphy and O'Connor laugh loudly in an almost hostile manner, almost jeering at their victory. Fred doesn't. He is too busy looking at The Girl With Yellow Hair, who is gulping her breath, near to tears, wiping her hand—the hand that touched the mouse—on the thick material of her skirt as she backs rapidly away.

"You think you're funny? Well you're not. You're just—you're just... –*horrible*!"

And because he is frightened and because he is upset, Fred starts laughing too—realising most of all, even though it might hurt the girl, that his laughter bonds him with the other boys, and that is far more important than what any *girl* might think. Isn't it?

Ignoring the taunts and poked tongues, Murphy dangles the mouse by the tail and drops it back into Parkhill's open pocket. They have achieved some victory. They have scared a girl, and it was fun.

Fred watches the females, long skirts, long hair, uniforms, stride away but only the one in pigtails looks back, briefly. He blinks. A frown is etched in her forehead. He wants to smile. He wants not to be nasty. It was a joke. He realises he *is* smiling, and he wonders why. He feels excited, too—and he wishes it could last longer. Much longer. Forever, in fact...

Then he realises Murphy and O'Connor are following Parkhill in the other direction, and he follows, upping his speed to catch up with them before they disappear round the corner.

"What happens to the mouse?" Fred asks.

"We kill it," Parkhill says, as if the remark hardly needed saying at all.

*

They emerge from a path beside some allotments and cross a stile into a field dotted with dandelions and tall weeds. O'Connor breaks a branch from a low-hanging tree and swishes it against the long grass. Fred snaps off another, briefly "sword-fencing" with him before O'Connor stabs him in the tummy. It hurts, but he doesn't say so. O'Connor holds his weapon above his head triumphantly, then slides in into a belt-loop of his shorts. Fred tip-toes around nettles. Hacks at a leaf with a ladybird on it.

The stone gateposts of an old house. One that has been derelict for years and has fallen into ruin. The windows are smashed or non-existent. There are no actual gates. In the overgrown garden, Fred and his mates kneel in a circle. Parkhill holds the mouse in his cupped hands. Each of the boys holds a house brick aloft.

Parkhill lets the mouse free on the ground between them and the boys madly attempt to clobber it—but the animal is too fast for them. It gets away. It's gone. They jump to their feet and rush around trying to find it, stamping, prodding with mossy sticks and dropping stones, lifting rolls of old carpet and heaving aside a rusty tin bath full of orange rainwater.

Fred just stands there. He thinks the mouse got away fair and square.

He isn't keen to catch it any more and he isn't sure he wanted to see it squashed and bloody in the first place. It didn't do any wrong. It was just a mouse.

Instead he turns and stares at the old house behind them.

His friends aren't watching. They're hunting.

Fred walks inside. He's a little bit scared. Just a little bit. But in another way it is really quiet and peaceful. He feels he is exploring like Dr Livingstone or Stanley and he feels he is being brave in a way that will make his friends like him and make his father proud of him. If there is fear in this house—this *haunted-looking* house—he wants to face it and prove to himself he *can* face it, because he is tired of trying to imagine what fear is like all the time, what it is like to be terrified out of your skin, and die of terror, of something so frightening your heart just stops. If it's going to happen, he'd rather get it over with.

In his polished black shoes he treads across the assorted debris, the broken plaster work and strips of wood layered in stone dust.

He looks up above him. Through the large holes where floorboards have caved in he can see into the shabby, abandoned rooms above.

He looks around him at the cracks in the walls, the wattle and daub exposed. The peeling paint of the door frames and fire surrounds. Outside he can hear Parkhill calling.

"Cocky! Cock! Where are you, mate?"

Fred doesn't answer.

He is looking at a filthy door with chipped paint. A plain door with a sliding bolt on it. He steps closer to it, touches the bolt. It's rusty, but with a bit of what his father calls "elbow grease" he pulls it back and yanks the door open.

He stares inside.

*

Lying in bed that night, eyes open and sparkling in his doughy complexion, he blinks away his thoughts of the house and the door as he hears footsteps and a voice outside his window. A woman's nervous laughter. A woman like his mother but not like his mother at all.

"No. No." Playful—then insistent. "No. No..."

He gets out of bed and goes to the window, clambering up onto his homework desk, pulling back the curtain and cautiously looking out, his breath clouding the cold glass of the pane. He rubs it away with his fingers.

Through the clear oval the street and night look cold and grey. It's black and white out there, like a film. A man and a woman, both in raincoats and hats, linger under the down-light of a street lamp. The man has his arms around the woman's waist. His head is nuzzling into her throat and cheek, a dog with a bone. She is pushing him away—but half-heartedly. In earnest one minute, then giggling the next.

"No! I said—*no!*"

The man embraces her more tightly—more *roughly*, forcing her body against his—and plants a long, unrelenting kiss on her lips. After it she separates from him, getting her breath back, then turns her back on him and walks away, a sway in her hips and her handbag dangling from her hand. He looks up unexpectedly, and sees Fred looking down at him.

Fred's spine stiffens. He hops back a few inches.

But the man grins. His chin bluish and unshaven. Still looking up at Fred, he makes his left hand into a fist and inserts his right index finger repeatedly in the hole he has created.

Fred swallows.

Grinning enough to show his teeth, the man pulls down his hat brim and lopes away after the woman, who has slowed down, clearly expecting him to follow her. Dawdling. So what she was protesting about Fred is at a loss to know. Was it a game? What sort of game? The sort of game he played in the playground with his friends? Do grownups play those games? What for? Fun? What kind of fun? And why did she say no when she meant yes? And why, after pushing him away, is she now hooking her arm around the man's?

Fred remains motionless, kneeling on his homework desk, trying to make sense of the gesture the man gave, the tight expressive movement of it, the vulpine glee in the night-eyes that went with it. Something upsets him about it and he doesn't know what. It was like stabbing. It was like hurting. It was like a wound. It was like Jack the Ripper.

He lets the curtain fall back, but before he can shrink away back to bed he hears whistling. Again from outside. Ululating from the brickwork. Some human nightingale. And a song that he knows intimately. Though it diverts from the melody quite a lot, pausing then trilling, the words can't help but go through his mind—he can't stop them...

A mother was bathin' her baby one night
The youngest of ten, the poor little mite
The mother was fat and the baby was fin
T'was nawt but a skellington wrapped up in skin...

Afraid what he might behold, but compelled to look just the same, he lifts the corner of the curtain again and peers out. The pane has started to mist up again but what he sees through it is all too clear...

The *policeman*—the very same sergeant of his incarceration no less—walks into the cone of light of the street lamp. Buttons glinting like stars against the night-black of him.

Fred hops back off his desk, landing on his feet, shuffling back quickly from the window until the bed hits the back of his knees, forcing him to sit on it. He presses his hands under his behind but he can't keep still. The invisibility of the policeman is somehow worse than the seeing of him, and he can't bear it. Because if he isn't out there—where is he? Inside the house? Outside the bedroom door? Why can't he hear the jaunty yet sinister whistling any more?

He jumps up again and scrambles back onto his desk on all fours. Not wanting to look but *having* to look, he plucks up sufficient courage— where from, he hasn't a clue, he isn't a hero, he isn't even a *man*— and bends his head round the curtain, pulling it taut with his hands, a shield...

The policeman pauses on his beat, hands behind his back, rocking back and forth on the balls of his feet, bending his knees in a slight squat. His truncheon dangles from his leather belt with its "snake" clasp. His eyes are buried in extreme shadow — grim, dark orbits of a skull on the Jolly Roger of a pirate ship. The strap of his helmet sits on the jut of his chin. The Brunswick Star on his midnight helmet glimmers. He blows into his cupped hands and rubs them together for warmth, but they remain white as chalk. As bone. Just up the High Street the bells of Saint John the Baptist (C. of E.) chime the hour — dull, solemn, funereal.

Fred jumps back, right onto the bed this time, with his knees in the air. He scuttles against the headboard and holds his breath, covering his mouth with his hand, convinced for a horrible minute that the policeman is coming to fetch him. That he is about to knock the door. That he is out there, looking up at the window the way the man with the stabbing finger looked up...

But why — why would he come at night-time? Why would he come *at_all?* Was it a "surprise raid"? Is that what they did with spies or suspected murderers? Did the sergeant have more evidence against him? Had somebody out there blabbed? Told lies about him? Perhaps his friends had. Parkhill. O'Connor. His so-called friends, that he trusted. And now...

But wait — can he be sure? The policeman hasn't knocked the door — *yet.* What is he waiting for? Is he waiting for Fred to give himself up? Come out with his hands up? Confess everything? Is *that* why he's here?

The little boy creeps back to the curtain. Hooks his fingers around the edge of it. Moves it gently, so gently, aside. Holding his breath...

The downward-pointing cone of lamplight is empty but for a duo of moths doing tiny figures of eight.

The policeman has evaporated, like the holy wafer on his tongue, into nothingness.

*

Not much but a crack of light gets in, even on a sunny day, and on a dull one it's like pitch. They know no-one looks here during school hours, and the priests *never* look here. They'd never get their hands dirty. They leave that to the caretaker. So this is where the gang go to be alone. The coal hole is their place. Their domain. Their den. It smells of soot and they have to blow their noses before they go home because their nostrils are full of black dust. It's dirty and Fred knows Father Mullins—old scrotum-face, as they call him—would say that's why it suits them, because *they're* dirty too. Nothing but *dirty, dirty* boys.

O'Connor and Murphy have a pack of cards and are playing Strip Jack Naked. Parkhill sits smoking a pipe. It's his grandfather's. There's no tobacco in it but it smells of rough Navy shag. Parkhill likes sucking it, believing it confers on him a wisdom beyond his years, and does so with great gravity, cross-legged, as he considers what Fred is reporting.

"He went like this." Fred repeats the obscene gesture of the man under the street light.

Inscrutable until now, Parkhill gives a grin from ear to ear.

"You know what that is?"

"What?"

"That's what your father does to your mother," Parkhill says, eyes narrowing with enjoyment, leaning forward for emphasis. "Puts his winkle in her whatsit..." Hushed now. "*Regina.*"

Fred is sceptical. "Don't be stupid!"

"I'm not being stupid. It's true."

"My father wouldn't do that."

"He would. They all do. They have to. They enjoy it!"

"Who?"

"Your father. *And* your mother."

"My mother wouldn't enjoy *that!*"

"Yer, she does." Parkhill's pipe jabs Fred's shoulder. "*And* they do it all the time. Not just when they want to make babies, either."

This is a serious revelation for Fred, and he disputes its veracity almost entirely.

"*I've* never seen them do it."

"'Course you haven't, you berk. They do it in secret, don't they? In bed. In private. It starts with kissing and that, usually."

Fred is confused, as well as appalled. "But you wee with it. That's what it's for. How can it be for—what you say?"

"It's why women and men are different. So they can fit inside each other." The end of the pipe is back clenched in Parkhill's teeth, springing erect as he pokes his right index finger into his left fist with the same jabbing rhythm of the man the night before.

Fred looks away. "You mean that's why God made them like that?"

"Well he did, didn't he?"

"But that's sin. Isn't it?"

Parkhill shrugs.

Fred asks, "Will we have to do it too?"

"If you want to have children you will."

"I don't."

"If you want a girl to love you, you do."

"No, I don't."

Fred stands up, wipes the coal dust off the rump of his shorts, to go back to lines before the bell rings. Parkhill shrugs that he can please himself but Fred doesn't care. He's heard enough nonsense and Parkhill is being stupid. O'Connor and Murphy look up, as if only just aware of the conversation, mainly because he is standing on their cards. They slap his legs. It doesn't hurt but Fred feels tears in his eyes a little bit and doesn't want them to see them because he's angry at them too. He's not sure why.

"You ask Father Mullins where babies come from," Parkhill pronounces as Fred lifts the latch on the door. "He'll tell you. They come from the hole between your mother's legs where your dad put his dickie in."

O'Connor and Murphy giggle.

"I know that." Fred looks back at him sternly. "*Everybody* knows that."

He pulls the coal house door shut after him.

*

In the lavatory cubicle, Fred unbuttons his shorts, standing at the toilet bowl.

He stares at the peep-hole in the wall. It has now been plastered over. Instead of weeing he buttons up his shorts and reaches over and touches the rough texture of the plaster with his fingertips. He turns round and sits on the toilet. Elbows on knees. Thinking.

Small, unevenly cut-up pieces of old newspapers hang up on a nail. He tugs one off but the nail falls out. He picks it up.

He places it in the palm of his left hand, a daring action occurring to him and instantly filling him with fear and trepidation. But also a compulsion that makes him feel quite excited at the prospect. The prospect of doing something he shouldn't.

He starts to cut into the wall of the stall with the point of the nail, using it like a tiny pencil, drawing a swift image in large, definite sweeps. Of a large, spouting penis and balls—the same crude graffito that he saw on the stinking wall of the horrid police cell.

He looks at it with some satisfaction. His mother often brags that he is "a good drawer" and here is the evidence—not that she will ever see it. He has reproduced the ferocious genitals exactly. It is quite an achievement. He realises his heart is beating hard in his chest and he swallows. He can hardly believe that he did it. He is proud of himself, but terrified. He thinks of the priests and the slap of the dreaded ferule. He thinks of his mother. He thinks of the policeman under the street lamp. He thinks of the squelchy, nasty gesture made by Parkhill and the man in the hat—even though he doesn't know why it worries him and makes him feel odd. He doesn't even know why he wanted to do it, but it's too late for that—he has.

He prods the nail back through the hole in the sheets of newspaper and presses it back into the wall, but it falls out onto the floor. He tries again but the nail falls out again, tinkling. This time he leaves it there. He stands up, pulls the chain of the cistern to flush it and leaves.

And the thing is this, he finds.

Once he is in the playground, nobody knows he has done an awful thing. The crime might be discovered, yes, but anybody might have committed it. There is no way for anybody to tell it was *him*. It is exciting in a way he didn't expect. It makes him feel like he knows what it is like to get away with murder.

*

The Yellow-Haired Girl who had been frightened by the mouse is walking along, a pair of ice skates slung over one shoulder.

"Leave me alone."

"I'm not doing anything," Fred says.

"Yes you are. You're bothering me."

"No I'm not."

"Yes you are." She turns to face him. "Go away."

He stands his ground. His inner terror is blatantly obvious, though he imagines it does not show. He is shorter than her and plumper than her. In every regard imaginable, it is an uneven match.

"This isn't the way you go home," she says.

"Sometimes it is."

"Where are your friends?"

"They're not my friends. Not really."

He has his hands in his pockets.

"What have you got in your pocket?"

"Something."

"A mouse?"

Fred opens one pocket slightly and looks in.

"It might be. ...Go on."

He's asking her to reach inside. She huffs. He must be joking if she'll fall for that a second time. Is he really that stupid?

"I see," he says. "You're scared."

"No I'm not."

"It might be something nice."

Of course, it might be. But…

She steps closer.

Her shoulders are square and she shows a certain bravado, but Fred can see she is tense inside. Untrusting. And why should she trust him? She shouldn't. But she doesn't know for *certain* there's something bad in there, either—and that's why he has her. The element of doubt. The element of doubt that one boy might not be as nasty as the last one. She's nobody's fool, and he likes that. She isn't pretending to be weak and watery and she isn't acting being scared so that somebody will look after her. She will look after herself. She's almost a boy like that. But she isn't *completely* a boy. She isn't *completely* safe. She isn't shy and she isn't mouthy and she isn't silly and she doesn't run away, but he enjoys the look of fear on her face. The look that wants to trust him but doesn't. Can't…

He nods.

Go on. It'll be all right. You'll see…

But will it? Will it be all right?

His stomach tightens as she forces herself to take another step closer to him in her ankle-length school skirt and lace-up boots. He senses her incipient bosom under the immaculately-ironed shirt.

She runs her tongue over her lips. Her eyes flicker. She swallows.

Go on…

She reaches into his pocket and retracts her hand quickly.

Though, wait. Nothing awful happened—her hand is still attached to her arm with no visible sign of attack. So she slides it inside, more confidently a second time. Wondering what is supposed to be there. Fingers spidering. Feeling around for it…

He watches her expression change. The fear dissipate. She looks at her palm.

"Empty. What was the point of that?"

Fred smiles.

"The point was, you did it."

She wrinkles her nose. "Very funny."

"Oh, sorry… It's in this pocket…" He rummages. Takes out a box of England's Glory matches. Holds it out to her. "Look inside."

"You must be joking."

"Open it. Please."

She carefully slides off the outer sleeve. And jumps with a SQUEAL— then almost immediately emits a honeyed, tremulous laugh that has the same effect on him as his mother's tickle.

In the matchbox is a child's thumb. A severed child's thumb, in cotton wool, with dabs of blood around it.

Fred extracts his own thumb from the hole in the box. Shows her how the trick was achieved.

"Why did you do that?"

"It's funny."

"No it's not, it's frightening."

"I thought it was funny. It made you laugh, didn't it?"

The Girl With Yellow Hair backs away, tilts her foot, swivels her ankle, walks away. Fred follows a few paces behind. She lets him, now.

"You know, you could kill people with those."

He means the ice skates.

"Why would I do that?"

"I don't know. No one would suspect the murder weapon. You'd get away with it. That would make a good twist."

"Twist?"

"That's a thing in a crime story you don't expect. Like the person who did it seems really nice, but they're not."

"I don't like to think about people not being nice."

Fred's mouth tugs down at the ends.

"I do."

They go up the steps to cross the railway line via an iron bridge over the tracks.

"Finsbury Park. Gillespie Road. Holloway Road. Caledonian Road. York Road. King's Cross. Russell Square. Holborn." He wonders why she laughs at him, but it isn't a nasty laugh, it's a nice one. "I know all the underground lines," he says. "And the bus routes."

"What's your name?"

He tells her.

The girl sniggers. She can't help it. "Itch. Cock. Itchy cock." She sees his intense embarrassment, and blushes. Just like he is doing already. "Sorry."

"I hate my name. What's yours?"

"Olga Butterworth."

"That's nice."

"No it isn't." She watches him pondering. "I'm not foreign. I'm English. My dad is from Lancashire and my mother's a Suffragette."

"Is she?"

Before she can answer, Fred hears a train chugging into the station below. Automatically, he takes out his note book and pencil to catch its number. Then double-takes and looks at Olga, who is smiling slightly. He fumbles to put it back in his pocket without writing anything inside.

As the train pulls into the platform underneath them, the billowing smoke rises from it like a great fog. It envelops them almost supernaturally, like a theatrical effect. Olga laughs. Unafraid of the supernatural, or of theatrical effects, and strangely, makes him feel unafraid too. But when the billowing clouds disperse, Fred sees that she has vanished, as if in a magic trick—just like his. He goes to the railing. Relieved to see her descending the steps on the far side.

He keeps watching as she walks from the railway bridge to the back door of a terraced house beside the railway track, leading into a small back yard. She shuts the door and a dog starts barking.

His eyes go up from the ground floor, where she enters, to the next floor up, where a bird cage hangs outside a half-shuttered window… to the next floor, where he sees Olga walk in and hang up her ice skates. In the little room her mother and father greet her. Olga laughs and demonstrates a little pirouette.

On the railway bridge, Fred looks down at something clutched in his little hand. It is the England's Glory matchbox. He takes out the inner tray and holds the hole up to his eye.

*

His mother swishes the blade of a carving knife and a sharpening iron back and forth vigorously. Her body jiggles. Her breasts and hips shudder under her clothing.

Fred sits at the kitchen table, a book in front of him. He turns to look at his father, who is seated by the fireplace in an armchair, one hand in a boot which he is blacking to a rare shine with a brush, dabbing it periodically in a one penny tin of Cherry Blossom.

His mother glides to the mantelpiece and winds the clock. One of her many onerous tasks. Fred watches her bottom, the taut lines from the waist of her skirt and the way they change as she moves. His father stops brushing and looks at the boy.

Fred puts his nose back in the book. Coughs. Then closes it.

"I've done my homework. May I go out and get some train numbers?"

His mother adds, "Please."

"Please."

Fred takes the silence for a yes. He heads to his room.

"Don't be late for bed."

The door closes. Her voice follows him.

Unseen by his parents, Fred kneels beside his bed. Pulls a case out from under it. *Up to no good* someone might say. The policeman might say. But he doesn't know whether it's good or not good, he just has to do it. And takes out a pair of binoculars and puts them in his satchel.

"Early to bed and early to rise makes a boy healthy, wealthy, and wise."

Fred's father looks at his wife who has spoken as the boy passes between them. A quiet man, who seldom finds that quality valued by many. Who sometimes thinks himself a freak of nature in the calamitous racket and rush of the new century.

*

Steam rises. He stands on the railway bridge. A train lingers on the platform below. But Fred's gaze—and the binoculars—are set on the back of the terraced house that Olga Butterworth calls her home.

The bird cage is being attended by an age-dappled old woman who is sprinkling bird feed through the bars.

He tilts the binoculars up.

Above, in a sitting room, Olga's father is wearing a fancy-dress black beard—a comical, ridiculous disguise.

In the room above that, Olga leans out of the window to peg out a pair of socks to dry. White socks. School socks. She pulls the curtains, then a gas light brightens, casting her silhouette on the hanging wall of cloth as she walks back and forth within.

He watches.

He is *there* to watch...

It's his job.

He wishes he could hear her voice.

He wishes he were closer.

The binocular lenses are fogged-up from the steam.

He cleans them diligently with a handkerchief wrapped round his first two fingers.

When he raises the object back to his eyes, there are other shapes cast on the curtain now—hand-shadows in the shape of a duck, then a rabbit...

Then the light dies like a vast disappointment.

*

Eyes fixed on the pavement ahead, he walks home past a large poster on a wall advertising the local skating rink, with a smiling woman sporting ice skates. He doesn't look up. It's later than he intended and he doesn't want to get a row. As he crosses the road he hears a hubbub of noise from the nearby pub. It becomes considerably louder when the doors open and two people are briefly regurgitated. A drunk woman in a second-hand fur coat is swaying, hardly able to keep upright, or even find her own mouth with her cigarette. She stops dead when she sees Fred staring over at her.

"Got a good eyeful have you, love?"

Fred can almost feel her rancid alcoholic breath in his face at twenty yards. There's laughter and Fred turns his head to see the equally drunk man in a bowler hat swaying on his heels, pissing at full flood in the doorway of a church. The flow of his urination, now trickling down the steps between his legs, would be the envy of a stallion.

Fred ducks his head down and walks away, his walk very quickly breaking into a run.

*

He reaches the doors of his father's grocer's shop, out of breath. The sign on the inside of the door says "CLOSED". Shooting desperate glances over his shoulder, he fumbles for his key. In his urgency to get inside he drops it.

It hits the ground and bounces, tinkling, towards a drain.

He falls to one knee, sprawls, snatching it up from the very edge of the gutter. Saved. Just before it was lost to the sewers.

He jumps to his feet, inserts it, turns it quickly in the lock, hurries inside, locking the door behind him.

He brushes the dirt off his knee and runs through the dark of the shop but forgets he has his satchel on and the satchel catches the edge of a box of apples which cascade onto the floor. Fred tries to stop them but it's too late. They are tumbling all around him.

"Who is it?"

Mother's voice, from above.

"Only me!"

Fred takes off his satchel and starts packing the apples back into the box on the trestle table. He collects them by the armful. Arranges them neatly one by one. He doesn't want his father giving him a look the next day with his beady eye. When he has done so to his satisfaction, he stands back to finally assess his work.

Hello?

He sees that a corner of the matting on the floor is turned up and there is something under it. Something—but, <u>what</u>?

Curious, he kneels down and peels the mat back further.

Under it is a brown envelope.

He takes it out, thinks a moment, looks around—stupidly—to see if anybody is watching (how could they be?) then hides it up his jumper.

He smoothes down the matting and presses it flat with his toe before venturing up the stairs. Dipping his fingers in the font as he passes, and genuflecting before Our Lady, but almost forgetting to.

*

"Where's Father?" He closes the door.

She sits reading a slim volume by gaslight. The Saint Francis picture flickers on the wall in its sepia glow. The birds seem to flutter.

"Gone to the pub." She closes her book—the Romantic poets—and pats the settee beside her. "Just the two of us. Just the way I like it."

"Mother, I'm tired. All those trains… And it's school tomorrow."

She pulls a sad face. Then makes a smile. But it's a sad one. It has to be.

He knows how this works and he has to ignore her or she'll get her own way. He has to be "not nice". He has to be like a man. He walks in the direction of his bedroom. His hand reaches door handle.

"Ah-ah!"

He turns around.

She points to her cheek.

He is duty-bound to come back and kiss it. It smells of Parma violets. He presses the flat of his hand to his tummy to hold the envelope there, in case she notices it.

"You don't have tummy ache, do you?"

"Me? No."

He backs away a few steps, smoothes his pullover flat, puts his hands behind his back. Turns. Goes.

"Don't forget your prayers, now."

*

Bare boards, hard seats, cheap beer. In the Public Bar of the Ten Bells, an assortment of drinkers laugh raucously at the spectacle before them. In the light of a crackling fire the policeman who locked up young Fred is carousing—that's the word, *carousing*—with the drunk woman. Her fur coat is on the floor and some loutish working men are standing on it with their big, filthy boots as they swig back the thin, brown liquid from their pint glasses.

The policeman occupies a stool by the grate and she is sitting, swivelling on his knee. He has the drunk woman's shoe in his hand and is holding it high over his head, out of her reach. She is trying to reach up and snatch it off him. She can't, but by doing so she is rubbing her body against his tunic. As she jumps in short, sharp jerks, her fingers stretching, her breasts are in his face. Her breasts jiggle.

Fred's father stands at the bar watching this.

Pairs of trousers surround her as she sways. The spectators ogle the entertainment like dogs on heat. Half a jug more and their tongues would be waggling. It's not often they get a show like this, that's for sure. A knees-up or a singsong round the Joanna and that's it. Where's the harm in it, eh? It's only a game. Only a bit of fun, innit? Cor blimey...

Fred's father finishes his beer and knocks back a chaser of whisky.

"That'll put hairs on your chest," says the barmaid.

He pushes the shot glass towards her, succumbs to a nod, meaning he'd like a top-up.

The barmaid shows him her back as she upturns the whisky bottle into the copper measure. He turns his head as he sees someone reflected in the etched bar mirror behind the array of bottles. He looks along the counter. The boy Parkhill is sitting on a tall stool behind the bar with a kitten on his knees, stroking it and drinking ginger beer from a bottle with a straw in it.

Parkhill sees him, and knows him, but doesn't smile.

Having emptied the second glass down his throat, Fred's father looks back at the policeman who is having a great time. Red faced in his uniform. Looking as if his collar might burst. Laughing and puffing on a fat, thick cigar that is wrapping both figures and audience in great gouts of smoke. The copper's tunic pulls at shiny buttons as he leans back on two legs of the stool. His belly, thrust out against the woman, threatens to pop them. And other buttons threaten to pop too. She doesn't find him even slightly odious. She runs her hands over his body, her white skin baby-soft against the black. The policeman's yellow teeth are exposed as he laughs and coughs cigar detritus. His tongue is layered and slug-like, eyes lost under puffy lids.

Fred's father imagines that a kiss is imminent, and turns back to the bar.

The policeman is repulsive, yet the woman hangs herself around him as if he is the most handsome man in London. He reminds Fred's father of some Roman Emperor at an orgy. A Nero being peeled a grape. Being pleasured by his concubine. He realises Nero is the only Roman Emperor he knows by name. His son no doubt knows the lot of them. His son could give him a list. With dates, probably. His son is good like that.

A cheer goes up as the woman closes her teeth around one of the brass buttons, threatening to bite.

*

He opens the brown envelope in bed. His heart starts beating faster. Inside he finds a small selection of saucy photographs. He knows the word *saucy* because O'Connor told him it once. Because he recognises a few foreign words he knows these are the kind made in a French photographic studio with nude models showing *all they've got*. The women, buxom, curvaceous, are striking exotic, theatrical poses. Chubby, rounded hips. Breasts cupped and offered in their hands. Peacock feathers in their hats—which is all they have on. Nipples like the suckers of the arrows he fires with his bow in the back yard. Ladies bent over with a coy finger to their chins, showing the camera the crack of their behinds. Curly hair falling loosely to shoulders, and other hair on display, dark and plentifully, below…

*

The policeman puts the drunk woman's shoe to his eye. He peers through a hole in it, eyeballing the other drinkers like a pirate through a telescope. The other male drinkers laugh uproariously.

Framed by the hole, the sergeant's iris is gigantic. His pupil dilated, engorged. His laugh rumbles from the cave of his chest and fills the pub with his presence, his dictatorship. Not that you could call it a laugh. Nothing of pleasure. The sound of a gravedigger's spade sinking into soil and bones.

*

He thinks of The Girl With Yellow Hair in her long skirt and lace-up boots. He covers the face of one of the nudes with the flat of his hand.

He catches his breath as he hears the gramophone in the other room start to play: a thin, high-pitched recording as an orchestra strikes up a spritely popular tune. Who is it? Who's there? Has somebody broken into the house? A thief? Have they come to get him? He's going to be caught red-handed! His bedroom door starts to open.

In a blur he hides the risqué photographs under his pillow.

The door swings open, slowly—wider…

From behind the half-open door a female leg graced with the diamond pattern of a fishnet stocking kicks in and out in time with the music.

For a bizarre moment he wonders, is it the policeman? In disguise?
Is it the woman from the police station with the hairs on the back of her
hand? Is it Jack the Ripper?

But no...

His mother saunters into the room trailing an umbrella as if on a
Sunday stroll, the fingers of one hand a platform under her chin. She
wears her petticoat over a short sleeved frock and a huge bonnet with a
big ribbon is perched jauntily on her crowning glory.

"I'm a young girl, and have just come over,
Over from the country where they do things BIG
And amongst the boys I've got a lover
And since I've got a lover, why I don't care a FIG..."

She sings with gusto, accompanying the trill voice on the recording
like the proper music hall *artiste* she imagines herself, in another life,
to be. Nailing every giddy "double entendre" despite her son's evident
lack of comprehension.

"The boy I love is up in the gallery,
The boy I love is looking now at me
There he is, can't you see, waving his handkerchief
As merry as a robin that sings on a tree..."

Fred grins with instant relief, but she thinks it is because he is adoring
it. Adoring *her*. But he is grinning because he has to. He knows. He's
her (captive) audience, of one—and it's not for the first time. Though
never at this time of night. Though never *wakened* for a performance,
'til now...

"The boy that I love, they call him a cobbler
But he's not a cobbler, allow me to state
For Johnny is a tradesman and he works in the Boro'
Where they sole and heel them, whilst you wait..."

Fred beams, feigning his enjoyment—no, feeling it, a little—as she
plays up the innuendo with saucy winks and big, pantomime gestures,
as she always does. What a turn! What a star!

"The boy I love is up in the gallery

The boy I love is looking now at me
There he is, can't you see, waving his handkerchief
As merry as a robin that sings on a tree!"

As expected, she ends on a big finish, arms flung wide. Face upturned to the Gods as the music ends and the trail of the gramophone needle renders a scratchy liturgy on the air.

"Bravo!" Fred applauds madly, kneeling up in his striped pyjamas.

In the glow of imaginary limelight his mother curtseys like a little girl. Exits stage left. (To take the record off the turntable.) Returning daintily for her all-important curtain-call. Soaking up the adulation. Every single grocer's weighing scale ounce of it.

"*Encore!*" Fred cries out till he's hoarse. "*Encore!*"

His mother sits on the end of the bed, getting her breath back. A modest hand resting lightly on her breast bone. Her chest rising and falling. He keeps on clapping furiously. Doesn't know when to stop. Daren't stop. Sometimes it seems no amount of applause is enough for his dear old mum.

Her hand doesn't move. Her eyes are on the floor. Her face darkens. Her mood slowly changes. He sees a mysterious pain cross her doll-white features.

"Stop. *Stop* it," she says curtly. Almost like a spit. Then catches his hands to immobilise them, as if the very applause she craves is now anathema to her, and unbearable.

Immediately she realises she was harsh, and is horrified—it was unforgivable, and she pats his little fists. She sits at the side of the bed. Takes his hand in hers and kisses them, full of remorse and utter self doubt. Making amends for something Fred doesn't even begin to understand, but feels like a dreadful and inexplicable ache.

Eyes shining in the semi-dark, she tucks aside a stray curl from his forehead. Looks into his face, sadly but lovingly. Desperate to ask something but afraid of the answer that might come.

"Do you think your mother's as pretty as an actress?"

"Yes. Of course," Fred says.

"Really and truly?"

"Yes, definitely. You're better than Marie Lloyd."

She laughs lightly. A half-caught breath. "And Florrie Ford?"

"And Florrie Ford!"

"Oh, you terrible boy!" First of all she sounds delighted, then she sounds bereft—full of heartache. "You terrible boy…"

She is thoughtful for a moment. She sniffs. Seems to be wiping away a tear. Then gets up quickly, turns the gas light down and walks to the door. A different person turns back.

"Your father'll want his bed tonight. You understand, don't you? It's time to be a big boy."

Fred nods.

His mother leaves the room, closing the door after her.

A few seconds later it eases open a few inches. She leaves it like that. The way he likes it.

And he lies back in his bed, head sinking into the pillow, staring at the ceiling. Thinking of the applause he gave. Thinking he would like it too, one day, for himself.

*

She wears earrings at the breakfast table.

"I've been thinking." His father dips a corner of bread in the yolk of his egg. "He should come on the cart today. Time he started learning his trade."

"There's no need for that." His mother eats her triangles of toast carefully with her finger tips. "He's destined for bigger things than being a *greengrocer…*" That last word sing-song of derision, insensitive to her own insensitivity.

"He won't go far wrong in life if he knows how to get his hands dirty."

They talk as if he isn't sitting between them. He looks from one to the other as they speak. But there is no more to say.

*

He follows his father through the shop. When he is sure nobody can see, he drops to his knees and swiftly takes the envelope of naughty photographs from under his jumper, slipping them back beneath the matting, where they belong.

*

His father holds the reins of the cart as the horse pulls it along at a steady pace. He wears a muffler round his neck tied in an untidy knot of which his wife would not approve. Fred sits next to him, hands neatly resting in his lap, mainly because he doesn't know what else to do with them. He feels like it's riding on a stagecoach in the cowboy stories he reads. Riding shotgun for Wells Fargo, protecting the U.S. Mail from marauding Apaches with paint over their bodies and feathers in their hair who might catch them and scalp them. Or bury them up to their necks in the sand and wait for the poison ants to bite and give them a slow and agonizing demise.

His father makes a click-clicking sound with his tongue. Flicks the reins and guides the horse over to the pavement. A Thomas Flyer beeps and overtakes him, its engine growling.

He hands Fred the reins.

Fred grips them tightly.

His father gets down from the cart and lifts a stack of vegetable boxes from the back.

Fred watches as he walks to a grocer's shop. The woman who owns it stands outside with her legs apart. She looks like she owns it, anyway, because she doesn't call out her husband. Perhaps her husband is dead. Perhaps she poisoned him. Put him in a barrel. A tin bath. A bag of potatoes…

She is big-busted and thin-waisted, with her hands on her hips and sleeves rolled up from tiny wrists. They exchange words chattily which Fred cannot hear as another car passes, rattling and tooting.

His father puts down the vegetable boxes, laughing easily with her which Fred thinks is not right. He doesn't laugh with his mother. He watches him strike a muscle man pose and the woman feels his bicep. She strikes a similar pose. He tickles her under-arm and she laughs not at all coquettishly. No play-acting. Earthy. As earthy as a man. Perhaps she *is* a man.

The horse snorts and shakes its mane.

Fred snaps out of his thoughts. Grips the reins for grim death. Locked in position. Hasn't moved an inch.

His father returns to the cart to lift off a sack of spuds which he carries to the shop.

Awaiting his return, Fred hears children's laughter and sees a couple of young lads, his own age but less well turned out than himself, running off at a clip that implies some nefarious deed. He turns to see what nefarious deed it might be.

The answer is instantaneous. One of the terraced houses has a front window with broken eggs running down it, the whites and the yolk combining into a rancid slime. Obviously the young guttersnipes responsible are now "legging it". The door of the terraced house opens and a woman rushes out into the street, looking right and left. But it is not a woman at all. It is the man dressed as a woman he saw in the police station. What shocks him more is that he or she is not well-off. He or she doesn't have a hat or furs. He or she is impoverished-looking, ill-clothed in a shabby dress and apron and garish face powder, making the stubble on his or her chin no less obvious, and ludicrously grotesque.

Fred ducks down slightly. Not wanting to be seen. Not wanting to be *remembered*.

Clearly upset, the man or woman cuts a gaudy, exotic and tragic figure as he or she disappears inside and returns with a wet cloth, mop and bucket to apply to the mess. Which is when he or she is aware of Fred, staring.

The boy looks sharply away, feeling the weight of the seat lurch as his father gets back up on the cart and takes the reins from him.

"Hup."

The cart moves off again and Fred fixes his eyes on the road ahead.

Behind him, the man or woman scrubs the pavement, presses the wet cloth in soapy circles to the window panes. Why was he or she in police custody, he can't help asking himself? What had he or she *done*?

But he doesn't look back—though he stiffens abruptly on the hard platform when he sees what is up ahead of him at the next street corner.

Because the policeman in the black moustache—the same one, the *very same one* who locked him up—has one of the young tearaways by the scruff of the neck, and is whacking him hard round the back of the head. The ragamuffin squirms, flinches, struggles, baby face contorting in distress, but the sergeant doesn't let go of him, literally lifting him from the ground, filthy bare feet dangling. A sprat held aloft by a fisherman proud of his catch.

The horse and cart trundles past the scene. Not quickly enough for Fred's liking.

Something of the sense of impending violence caught in a single moment reminds him of the posed figures at Madame Tussaud's Chamber of Horrors, with the policeman as the murderer and the child as his victim. He could have a carving knife in that hand he's not showing behind his back, ready to cut the urchin's throat. Ready to *dispose of him...*

The scruffy kid wriggling in his iron grip, the copper finds himself distracted momentarily as he recognises Fred's father. He straightens his back, almost forgetting the dangling perpetrator of the ghastly crime while the impoverished whippersnapper dangles like a hanged man from a noose. Like Charlie Peace.

"That boy of yours behaving himself, Mr H.?"

Fred's father does not looking at him directly.

"Oh yes."

"He'd better be!" the policeman says. "Or I'll have a bone to pick with you!"

And as Fred's father drives the cart on past the Keeper of the Law drain-laughs, belly taut behind his belt, like it is the most wonderful joke imaginable. And keeps on laughing. Like it is the best joke ever told in the history of the world.

*

The organ drones the *Agnus Dei* (God's little lamb) in the chapel of Saint Ignatius as Fred performs his duties as an altar boy. Preparing the Holy Communion, lighting candles, opening the book of prayer, holding it so the priest can read from it with the minimum of personal effort. The priest in question being the formidable and fearsome Father Mullins.

Old bollock-features.

The elderly man mouths his words with his usual saliva-spraying zeal, but today Fred doesn't hear a single one of them. He has more important things on his mind.

*

"Now then, Hitchcock. I hear you have some questions you want to ask."

"Yes, Father."

Mullins sits behind his desk in a study armoured by books. He gives a gracious wave of the hand as if to say "Proceed".

"Father... How do you know if you've got bad thoughts or not?"

Father Mullins has a hard-boiled egg on a plate. He cracks it and starts peeling the shell off it.

"Well, ask yourself what God would think. Ask God."

"How do I do that?" Fred says. "Where is he?" "Everywhere."

"Isn't he a person then?"

"No, of course he's not a *person*. He's Maker of Heaven and Earth. Father, Son and Holy Ghost."

"That's three people," Fred observes.

"No, that's one. One Trinity. That's what that is. He's all around us, as I say, in different forms."

"I can't see him."

"Ah. That depends how hard you're looking. If you look, thou shalt find. Look for instance in your own heart. Look there. That's a decent place to start." The Jesuit bites one end off the hard boiled egg and masticates.

"What if he's not there?"

"If he's not there, you're in trouble." Father Mullins pours salt in a little triangular mound on the side of his plate.

"What kind of trouble?"

"I don't know. Do *you* know?"

Fred shakes his head. Sighs.

"I'm confused, Father."

"Well, don't be. Don't be at all, in the slightest. All you have to remember is, He died for our sins."

"But didn't He commit a sin in the first place?"

"How d'you mean?"

"Well, Mary had a boy child—God's son, Jesus. That was a sin."

"How d'you make out that? How was it sinful? It was within wedlock. She was married. To Joseph."

"But Joseph wasn't the father, was he? So Mary sinned. With God."

Father Mullins shifts in his seat, uncomfortable. His hand waggles in the air in front of him.

"Look, this is not the kind of thing you need to worry about at your age. Believe me. It isn't."

"But Jesus was crucified as a criminal. For a crime he didn't commit. What was the crime they thought he committed?"

Father Mullins emits a long, quiet, mewling sound.

"It's... *complicated*."

"And why did God allow him to be punished and hurt like that if he was his father and loved him?"

The old priest coughs. His throat is unaccountably dry, all of a sudden. Possibly the egg. "It's—it's extremely—*com-plex...*"

"Why didn't his father help him?"

"Well, there you have it." The chair soughs under the old feller's weight as he rocks back. "That's the eternal mystery. Of our inability to understand Christ. And—and, and, and God. Because—because we are merely, you see, *human beings*." His eyes swim limpidly in his bollock face. "Does that answer your question?"

Fred doesn't think it does. Not at all. Not really.

"I just..."

"Look, all you need to know is he died for our sins, all right?"

"Why?"

"You don't need to know *why*. For Heaven's..."

The Holy Father has had enough. The hard-boiled egg, yellow and white, rests on the plate, half-eaten on its china Golgotha.

Fred looks no less troubled than he did before the discussion began.

"Will I find out if I become a priest?"

"Will you what? Do you *want* to become a priest?"

"Yes, Father," Fred says. "Yes, I think I do."

"Why's that, in the name of God?"

Fred thinks for a moment, staring at the desk, the fountain pen, the blotter, the hard, claw-like hands riven with the blue cables of veins.

"Because if you're a priest, you're innocent," the boy says.

*

"Lars Porsena of Clusium
By the Nine Gods he swore
That the great house of Tarquin
Should suffer wrong no more..."

He sits at his small wooden desk, idly playing with his nib pen, pressing his fingertip to it to see how sharp it is. His friend, the willowy reed O'Connor, is standing in front of the class reading in Macaulay's *Horatius* from a poetry book in a drone absent of both conviction and understanding.

"By the Nine Gods he swore it,
And named a trysting day,
And bade his messengers ride forth,
East and west and south and north,
To summon his array…"

The dullness of the words lulling him to the point of hibernation, he presses the nib of the pen into the palm of his hand. For no substantial reason except to feel something—anything—he tests it with idle curiosity against the soft flesh.

Ouch! It hurts!

He puts the pen down in the ridge next to the inkwell and folds his arms tightly, praying no child or master has seen the action of such a nitwit.

*

Their grey duffel coats billow behind them like cloaks, sleeves knotted round their necks. Parkhill, considered the leader especially by himself, turns and mimes fencing with Murphy, who is easily defeated by the most dangerous swordsman in the whole of France. *Voilà, pig dog!* He sees Fred joining in, corkscrewing his own rapier, free hand aloft and limp.

"Oi. What do you think you're doing?"

"*En garde!*" Fred stops, arms hanging, matching the other boy's pose. "What? What have I done wrong?" He always assumes he has done wrong, and he is usually right.

"I said we were playing *The Three Musketeers*." Pulling a sour face, Parkhill points at the other two, then himself. "One. Two. Three."

"Yes, but there were four musketeers in the book." Fred states his case. "There was D'Artagnan too."

"Don't be stupid! It's called *The Three Musketeers*, idiot."

Murphy and O'Connor snigger.

"Yes, I know. But I'm right. There was Athos, Aramis, Porthos…"

"*Four* Musketeers? *Twerp!*"

The minions snigger some more. Fred knows they will not listen to reason. They will listen to Parkhill. They have never read the book, and neither has he: Fred wants to tell them that. That they're stupid. He wants to tell them he is smarter than them, but he can't. He can't because even though they're wrong if he persists he thinks they will stop liking him. So instead he stands there mutely as they laugh at him, cheeks flushing red with rage and hurt—but mostly hurt.

"Come on, you lot." Parkhill swivels on his heel to Fred and jabs a finger at his face. "Not *you!*—Buzz off!"

Fred watches them scamper across the road, exuberantly swishing at each other with sweeps and thrusts of imaginary swords, letting off a round from an invisible flintlock pistol, clutching a flesh wound that then, miraculously, disappears.

He tells himself he didn't want to play their stupid game, if their idea of accuracy is so lax. You know where you are with books. Books are the same every time you open them. Every time. But people aren't. Boys aren't. And he hates that. Hates them. Because he wanted to be brave and courageous just like they did, and now what is he, his chest rising and falling as he holds back stupid, girlish tears? The kind of tears that would get him thrown out of the Musketeers, that's for certain. In his mind he thrusts his rapier through their hearts, one by one. *One, two, three.* Sees the rose of blood opening as the blade comes out. The look of bewilderment coming over their features before they crumple to the ground.

"Hello."

Fred turns. "Hello." He should put his weapon in its scabbard, he thinks.

It's Olga Butterworth. Milady. The mysterious. The fair.

"Are you crying?"

"No."

"Come here."

She sounds soft. Nice. Like a friend. A better kind of friend. He walks over to her, not sure why. His chest—the feeling inside his chest—is still funny. Crushing but fluttering. Funny. Not funny ha-ha, funny strange.

She takes out a handkerchief. At the sight of it he backs away, recoiling from a possible blow.

"Please yourself." She sounds hard again.

She turns and walks away. He desperately un-knots his duffel coat sleeves from his neck, ties it quickly around his waist, and catches up with her.

*

They sit on a bench half-way along a path beside a hedge. They are facing allotments. Beetroot patches. Bean poles. Paltry scarecrows in old, torn shirts. One has an army cap on its head, tilted at a jaunty angle. Fred takes a comic from his school satchel and hands it to her.

"You fill in the spaces and they add together to make a story. It's great fun."

She gazes at the cover. "*Plotto*."

She's as little enamoured with the title as she is with the concept, he can tell. He watches her leafing through it, feigning interest to spare his feelings. At least she thinks of his feelings. Which is something. Isn't it?

"Do you want to go to the pictures?" he asks.

"Don't you need to go home?"

He shakes his head.

"Won't you get into trouble?"

Fred shakes his head.

"I can stay out as long as I like," he says. "I do it all the time."

"What? All night?"

"If I like."

"You won't get a hiding when you get in?"

Fred shrugs. "I don't care."

"What if your mum and dad complain to my mum and dad?"

"They won't."

"They might."

"They won't."

Olga hands him back the *Plotto* comic.

"Did you see *Scenes of the World*? I've seen it nine times," he says. "It shows scenes of The Black Hills of Dakota, and Monument Valley, with those whopping big rocks in it. That was great, but my favourite was *Ride on a Runaway Train*. The camera was mounted on the front of the engine car as it whizzed around the mountains... you'd never believe it! When it took a bend it made you go like this!" He leans over to one side. "Then like *this!*" He leans over even further in the other direction. "And it was under-cranked so it made it look even faster... plunging into a tunnel—and *you* plunging with it!"

Olga grins. The boy's enthusiasm is infectious.

He grins too. "The owner of the picture hall puts sheets of newspaper down because they get so many wet seats!"

She laughs. Fred likes the sound of it very much.

"The Theatre Royal on Salways Road is showing a new animation," he says.

"I haven't got sixpence."

"I've got a shilling. I can get us both in."

She is still smiling and he takes comfort in that, but it makes him feel guilty too, because he knows what he is thinking deep down and she doesn't. That is the whole point—*she doesn't*. His heart is beating faster as she stands up and begins walking back the way they came, lifting the hem of her skirt from being soiled by the mud of the path.

"No. This way," he says, keeping his smile in place. "It's quicker."

*

Ahead of him, her hands push back a branch and a curl of brambles, right and left. She walks past the stone gate posts with the derelict house beyond. It is all going exactly according to the plan. Exactly according to the plot. Just like *Plotto*. If he was a thief or a spy he couldn't have planned it better. Or if he was a murderer.

He drops to one knee to do up his shoe lace. Not that it needs doing up. But it makes her stop and turn back to look at him, as he knows it will. And when her eyes are on him, he walks through the space where the gates used to be, into the overgrown garden beyond.

"What are you doing?" she says. "Come back."

"Do you know who lived in this place?"

"I don't know anything. I just want to go."

Fred looks back at her, puts down his duffel coat and satchel, then walks into the building.

"Get out of there! Somebody said there's a tramp living inside!"

"That's just a story."

The room is as it was the first time he stepped into it. Run to ruin. The discarded corpse of a room. A murder mystery waiting to be solved. It is slatted with shadows, a place that reeks of night even though the sun shines outside. An English sun, so that's not saying much. But he's not afraid of the dark. Not any more. Edgar Allan Poe and Robert Louis Stevenson have shown him there are worse things to worry about. They've educated him with apple barrels and Ben Gunn and eyes under floorboards and the police rapping at your door. He is safe because he is in charge here, away from the sun. He will make sure he is.

Full of trepidation, Olga follows him in. Fair maid. Damsel in distress. Not yet she isn't.

"This is mad, this is. I'm going. I'm going to leave you here."

"Don't," says Fred. "Stay."

"Why should I?"

"There's something I have to do. I have to do it to prove I'm not scared…"

"What are you talking about?"

"You'll see."

"'I'll see?' What will I see?"

Fred approaches the door he approached before. He loosens the rusty bolt with some effort and yanks it back.

Olga covers her ears—the groan and screech is loud.

Fred creaks open the door and looks inside. He recoils with a sharp intake of breath and takes a few steps backwards.

Olga rushes over and cuts in front of him, so that she can see what he saw. She stiffens, prepared for some kind of shock. But all she does is frown.

In front of her is nothing but a broom cupboard, with nothing in it—not even a broom. All she can see is skirting board and chipped paint and a few hooks on the wall. She releases her fear in the gasp of a laugh.

In the same moment she feels a weight against her from behind and finds herself shoved forward, neck cricking back and legs buckling. Her head hits the far wall as she flounders, grasps, bewildered, the rest of her sprawling against it.

Fred slams the door shut and swiftly closes the rusty bolt.

Plunged into immediate darkness, Olga scrambles quickly to her feet and starts pushing against the door from the inside.

Fred backs away from it, arms hanging vertical at his side. His smile has vanished. The mask of it has gone and he feels bad at the deception. But a clever spy, thief, murderer—where are they without deception? Without a smile that isn't a smile?

He jolts as the door shudders at the force of Olga's fists on the other side of it. He blinks furiously. The rusty bolt rattles and vibrates but does not give.

He bunches his little fists as he hears her get her breath back. He swallows, his feet fidgeting in little wee steps to and fro. Stop it, stop it—but too late now to stop anything.

"What are you doing? Fred?"

"Nothing." He's backing away further from his deed, stiffened with panic.

"Can you let me out please?"

"I will."

"Do it then."

"No. I can't."

And he knows, literally, that is true.

"Fred…"

"I don't want to. Not yet. Don't ask me to."

"Fred, why are you doing this?"

"Because. I don't know. I just have to."

"Why?"

"Because you committed a crime. You know you did."

She laughs. Mystified. "What?"

"You might not think you have, but you have. I know you have. I know everything."

"You've lost your marbles, you have. Now, let me out of here before you're in trouble!"

"*I'm* not in trouble. *You're* the one in trouble, Sonny Jim!" Fred's voice is shriller than he would like. "You're the one *going to Hell* if you're not careful!" The words are the best he can muster for the purpose. He wants her to be terrified. He wants her to feel awful. He wants her to sob her blinking heart out—but to his alarm she emits a different sound entirely. "Stop. Stop it! What are you laughing at? You won't be *laughing* down there, I can tell you! Not down there in hell with your knickers burning. With your knickers burning *right off* showing all you've got—you won't be *laughing* then, will you?" He wants to be evil. He *is* evil. He knows he is.

As he holds his breath, the wetness of spittle on his lips, Olga goes quiet. Good. He's seething. Good!

"Don't be a bugger, Fred! Listen to me. Don't be a bloody bugger!"

"I will! I *will* be a bloody bugger! You'll see!"

And he's frightened—*he* is frightened, *and* enjoying it too. And thinks of his mother seeing him like this, not her dear little lamb with its fleece white as snow, oh no, not that any more, a man—a nasty creature, a creature getting pleasure from tears and distress and feeling good about it. Yes! Feeling good about it. Feeling strong. Feeling the strongest person in the world, who will never get pushed around ever again. That's what he feels like. And the more the girl suffers, he thinks, and perhaps knows, even then, the more he will like it.

He turns and runs. Out of the room. Out of the house. Feeling the warmth of the sun again—English sun, no sun at all, the warmth being the blood pumping under his skin—and hears her squawking from within.

"Fred! Fred! Let me out! Let me out!"

But no. He doesn't. Can't. He picks up his duffel coat—scratchy, hairy, grey—from where he left it in the Dead Garden of broken tiles and twisted plants, and walking between the mildewed gate posts he cannot hear her any more. She is not Olga Butterworth. She is The Girl With Yellow Hair. She has to be, because he invented her. She is inaudible. Invisible. As if shut away in the pages of a closed book. A story only he knows, because he wanted to tell it. Tell it his way, this time.

His.

*

He slows down to avoid attracting attention but risks a smile. Straightens his back to look less furtive. Flattens his cow's-lick with fingers wetted by his tongue. A shop assistant (name of Kidney) ratchets in the awning above the windows with a hooked pole.

Inside he is safe. Inside he is a little boy again.

*

A kettle whistles on the stove. His father fills a hot water bottle with boiling water, careful to press it against his chest to expel excess air as he does so. Accidents can happen. The hidden dangers of household chores are numerous. It's a job a husband does not leave to his wife. That's the way they apportion their lives—in tasks. He feels the heat against his chest. Feels the hot breath coming up against his face from the open rubber mouth. His nostrils quiver.

*

Jesus Christ peers out from the Sacred Heart, as real as a scene from the Roxy, the flickering of the gaslight giving a sense of a hidden projector or magic lantern. The anticipation of a story to be told or a parable to be learned.

Fred lies flat as a corpse in his bed, arms ramrod straight outside the covers. Eyes open wide, his breathing uneasy—neither for the wanting it. What terrifies him he cannot say. No one can know. No one can see.

The door opens and he flinches. Twists his head. He doesn't know who he expected—Jesus? Jack? Ripper? Redeemer?—but his father steps into the room. He hands Fred the hot water bottle, which Fred tucks down into the bed, manipulating it right down to his icy feet.

"Not reading?"

Fred shakes his head.

"Wonders will never cease." The greengrocer does not rest on his son's eyes. He hardly ever does, and neither of them knows why. "I'm taking your mother out for a nightcap. Will you be all right on your own for an hour?"

Fred nods. He knows he will have to be.

The man drifts to the bedroom door.

"Father? What's a spy?"

"A person who keeps secrets. Somebody who says he's one thing but he's really another. Why?"

"I just wanted to know."

His father silents out of the room, sliding the door shut after him.

*

In the broom cupboard her face is barely picked out in a string of moonlight. She tries to poke through at the bolt and move it using the pin of her hair clip—tortoise shell with rams' heads, influenced by the excavation at Nineveh by Sir Henry Layard. The pin head scratches ineffectively. Uselessly. It's frustrating and she expels a sound of that frustration. A snarl.

After a breath she tries yet again. The pin snaps off.

This sends her insane in a short, sharp burst—banging her fists at each of the three walls, tearing at the door with her fingertips and kicking at it hysterically.

This also does No Good Whatsoever.

She now knows her physical efforts are useless. She has been at it for hours. She crouches down then sits, with her arms around her legs. All school skirt and socks both like sacking, dirt and a cut on her face where she hit the wall, hair tousled and messy without the hair grip. She gives in to a cascade of sobs.

"Help! Help me! Help me! Mum! MUM!"

Loud enough for insubstantial lungs, but quite futile.

Nobody can hear her. Nobody is listening. Nobody cares.

The ruined house is dark. Outside it, not a sound sails on the night air except for a distant train rattling melodiously on its tracks, oblivious to the petty anguish of a child.

*

The two worlds are separate. Standing at the bar of the pub, waiting to order drinks, Fred's father can see into the other half—the Public Bar—noisier and far more barbarian than the Saloon Bar he is in himself. The Saloon Bar is the place a businessman frequents. A place a man can safely take his "lady wife" without there being any fear of her feminine sensibilities being affronted. The Public Bar is a sawdust-strewn den of beer breath, unshaven chins and language that would make a costermonger die of shame. He'd perhaps have gone there tonight, or any night, on his own. He doesn't mind mixing with working men—even though she says he ought not to. But tonight is different. Tonight she is in charge. It makes him tense, but he has to endure it as best he can. Though he will be happy when it's over.

He sees another moustache opposite, for a moment like his own reflection emerging from the miasma of the uncouth. His "friend" the policeman—if he *is* a friend – is getting a pint. The black uniform falls like the shadow of a tree. The sergeant sees Fred's father and brightens markedly, heading round to the side-door to meet him. Fred's father isn't terribly pleased about that.

The copper enters from the Public Bar, a Goth invading Rome. He is used to owning a room and swivelling heads, in his professional capacity of course. Relishes it, in fact. He isn't cowed by the cushions and furnishings absent from where he came from, or by the presence of solicitors and shop-owners with their straight backs and sherries. He is as good as them, if not better. King or commoner, none of them is above the Law, and he *is* the Law. And knows it.

And wait. Fred's mother, done up to the nines, white cotton gloves, the lot.

"Well, well. *Enchan-tay*, as they say in gay Paree!" He takes her hand and kisses it. Fred's mother bends away from him, acting coy but flattered by the attention. His grin slobbers over every inch of her. "Good to see you taking in London's good air, Mrs H.—eel and pie air that it is. Some people round here thought you didn't want to be seen down here with us *low types*."

"Perish the thought," she says. "We are all equal in God's eyes, Stanley."

"Well, here's to God, and all who sail in him!" He pulls up a stool. Closer than she would like. Or perhaps not. Fred's father returns to the table with a drink for himself and his better half.

She pulls the drink towards her. "The time has long gone when it was considered a scandal for a respectable woman to drink in a public house."

"Are you a respectable woman, then, Mrs H.?" The policeman would wink if he needed to.

"As my husband is a notable figure in the community," she says, "I like to show my face."

He points to her drink. "Few more of those, duck, and that's not all you'll be showing."

She blushes with shock, but enjoys the frisson of the innuendo. Fred's father pretends to, but his smile is a tired one.

"You are a one. He's a one, isn't he, William?"

"He's a one, all right."

"In the words of the prophet Isaiah: 'A little of what you fancy does you good.'" The dark sergeant sluices back his beer. Fred's mother hides her canary titter behind her hand. Fred's father empties his glass in the same long, slow swig as the other man.

Still grinning, the shadow with buttons rises and sidles to the bar to order more, not asking if anybody wants more. Just doing it, whether they want it or not.

*

Mice crisscross the floorboards. From behind the door of the broom cupboard in the mausoleum dark, a weak, irregular knocking emanates.

Mum. Mum. Mum. Mum...

*

Deep in the comfort of his pillow, Fred turns to lie on his side, staring hard at the Sacred Heart on the wall. He wonders if Jesus is just a policeman in the end, a policeman of Right and Wrong. He wonders if He can see into his soul and what He can see there, because Fred doesn't know what is there himself. He really doesn't.

Really he wants to cry inside, but he can't.

What *is* he inside? In *his* heart? Is he what the policeman said he was? Don't adults always know best? *Do* they, though?

The hot water bottle has lost its warmth and with it has gone his panic and the sense of dread of being found out. But he thinks of how cold the girl's feet are. He thinks of being there, touching them, warming them.

He thinks of her allowing him. And closes his eyes.

He wishes he could turn the clock back. He doesn't like being a criminal. He didn't find it easy and it doesn't come naturally. There are too many feelings and he'd prefer to lock those feelings out. He was better off without them. He wishes he could understand feelings like he understands bus timetables and tram routes, but feelings don't stick to planned routes, before you know it they are zooming off in all sorts of directions. But for the first time, also, he thinks he knows why a murderer does what he does—because he really, *really* likes it, that's why, because it makes him feel superior: to the police, to the mothers and fathers, to the priests, to everybody. Even to God.

He stares at the Sacred Heart again, thinking of what Christ went through and wondering why He can smile like that. He thinks of The Girl With Yellow Hair and her suffering too—the girl who was kind to him and let him into her (sacred) heart. And the strangest thing is that he thinks he should feel something, and he tries to, but he feels nothing at all.

*

In the Saloon Bar more alcohol has been downed. The policeman has sunk quite a few and now stares at the floor, eyes glazed, with ale-froth icing the tips of the hairs of his grand moustache. Coarse laughter washes in from the Public Bar and Fred's mother cringes as if it's agony to her delicate ears.

"My father was a bobby on the beat," she says in her brogue, laid on thick for his benefit. "West Ham. P.C. Whelan. Fine figure of a man."

"I'm sure he was," the policeman says, eye rolling over her corset-bound curves.

"You know, over there they have no respect for the law. No respect at all. Spat at in the street, he was—every day of his life. Had to turn the other cheek."

The policeman empties the bitter brown liquid from his glass down his gullet. "Spit? Bit of *spit* he had to put up with, did he?" Wiping his lips with his cuff and sucking his teeth. Face hard and sour, as if tasting something putrid off them. Smile gone and heaviness now upon his eyelids. "Face bullets, did he? Face *spears*, did he?"

Fred's mother frowns at the strangeness of the question, and the cold change that comes over the Life and Soul of the Party.

"That's what I've had to face," the pitch moustache says. "Flying column from Wadi Halfa. Heroes of the hour. Oh, yer. 'Cept the bleedin' Mahdi already had Gordon's head on a spike, didn't he? Dervishes to the right of them. Dervishes to the left of them... The hordes of Hell, I've had to face. The black hordes of Hell." In the yellow splutter of a match he strikes, his face looks as monstrous as something that belches water from the gutters of a church roof. Something carved to ward off bad spirits. Or a bad spirit itself, in human form. Every ounce of humour miraculously shed.

"That boy of yours." His head lolls. "Wait for him to kill somebody. That'll make him grow up. That'll make him grow up all right."

Fred's mother isn't amused by her attentive admirer any more. She's upset, and perhaps that's as he wanted it all along—she doesn't know and doesn't care, but doesn't like to be made a fool of. She looks to her husband in desperation, who sees the signs right enough. The noise, everything, too, too much. His wife is no longer happy and gay—that was too vain a hope. Not for the whole evening. She looks frightened. A doe that intuits the arrow of the hunter. Alert yet bewildered, as if she might faint.

"Come on." Fred's father has her. No fear. "Let's take you home."

She stands unsteadily. Neck tall and proud, like a swan. Her husband tucks her arm under his and they leave. And if they leave the policeman yawning and licking his dry mouth, murmuring laughter to himself at their expense, they pretend not to see him, or care.

*

Concentric circles ripple in the tiny font. The back room of the shop is in darkness and the guffaws and sing-song on the night air long vanished, but the piano, that torture instrument, still hammers on her nerves. Her husband takes her coat and hangs it up, before his own.

She sinks at the table. Takes out her rosary beads and turns them over in her hands as he pours and hands her a glass of water.

"Leave me be."

Her dogged husband waits.

"Leave me be."

He turns and trudges to the wooden stairs. Weary in more ways than he can begin to tell. She unexpectedly speaks again, as if this thing could not be said to his face, only to his back, and even then in shadow.

"Am I a good person, Bill? ... *Am* I?"

He stops.

She closes her eyes tightly, clasping her hands together in prayer and sobbing quietly as she prays. The scripture pours out of her in a rush. It can't come fast enough.

Her Bill, William, sits down across the table from her and takes her hands, separates them, kisses them each, one by one. She cannot understand his affection. It is the greatest mystery to her. He wishes it wasn't.

They look into each other's eyes. Too many questions ever to ask.

She through tears, and trembling.

*

"They fought the dogs, and killed the cats
And bit the babies in the cradles
And ate the cheeses out of the vats
And licked the soup from the cook's own ladles..."

As he reads, book open to Browning, Fred notices Father Mullins— old bollock-features—enter like a ghost and whisper into the ear of the young priest facing the class. He wonders why. He wonders what...

"Split open the kegs of salted sprats…"

The young priest nods. The soutane of Father Mullins, mummified skeleton inside, yaws from the room like the black sails of a funeral barge.

"Made nests inside men's Sunday hats
And even spoiled the women's chats…"

No sooner does the door close than it re-opens and he returns with a police officer at his side—not just *any* police officer, but with awful inevitability the dread figure of Fred's incarceration. Helmet tucked under one arm. Giant in a realm designed for boys. Black standing beside black. A dark duo. And Fred feels the air sucked out of him but dares not stop breathing or reading aloud however much he wants to.

"By drowning their speaking
With shrieking and squeaking
In fifty different sharps and flats…"

The young priest waves his hands, gesturing Fred to stop and sit. Fred does so. Happily. If not happily, obediently. Obedience being second-best to invisibility—which is what he wants now more than anything. Murmurs of apprehension and excitement circulate around him. Rising in volume.

"Silence. *Silence!*"

Silence is thereby imposed in an instant.

"Boys." Father Mullins addresses them with no glimmer of warmth, the turkey-scrag of his neck rubbing the dog collar as he scans every face. "Sergeant Sykes is going to address you on a very serious concern. And I expect—nay, I *demand* you give him your *complete* attention—is that clear?"

In unison: "Yes, Father."

Mouthing the words, Fred can hear his heart drumming so ferociously he thinks they all must hear it too. His tell-tale heart. The one under the floorboards. The one inside his ribs. Wanting to be let out.

The policeman places his helmet on the desk beside him, badge gleaming, blinding like the Sacred Heart, and stands in front of it. The blackboard squeals in protest as it is wiped. Hands behind his back, he rocks back and forth on his heels and the schoolboys can hear the squeak of his polished boots as he does so. The crease in his trousers is sharp enough to slice a Sunday roast. His chin juts out like a prow.

"Now then." The growl. "Any of you lads know a girl named Olga Butterworth?"

A solitary (tell-tale) bead of sweat trickles down the nape of Fred's neck.

The boys look at one another. The former musketeers—Parkhill, O'Connor and Murphy—look at one another, then at Fred. Fred dare not look back at them.

"She goes to the Convent School next door."

"These boys do not consort with Convent School girls, Sergeant." Father Mullins says emphatically. "We're very strenuous on the matter. *Very* strenuous."

"If you say so," the policeman says. Taking nothing as gospel, he scans the boys at their desks.

Fred does not want to look into those steely eyes. Doesn't want them cutting into his soul. And that's what *he* wants, isn't it? To cut them open and see what's inside. What's going on in their minds. To know what they've been up to. What they've been dreaming, the butter-wouldn't-melt little tykes...

Fred being one of them. With more to hide than most.

A lot more.

He stares at the floor. Tightening his little fat fists to stop from shaking. To stop from shouting out loud: *It's me! It's me!*

"She went missing last night," declares the policeman with a commanding authority beyond even that of the Holy Brothers. "Her parents were expecting her home at tea time. If any of you know of her whereabouts, or saw anything at all suspicious, I'd ask you to report it immediately to either me or Father Mullins."

"You hear that?" the aging Jesuit repeats. "Immediately!"

But for now nothing is forthcoming. Not a movement. Not a whimper.

What *could* be forthcoming, Fred thinks, since the only person with anything forthcoming is himself?

"Don't worry about getting into trouble," the sergeant adds. "Or getting anyone else into trouble. You won't. You'll be doing good." His eyes fall on Fred and he doesn't recognise him instantly, but after a second he does. *(Bill Hitchcock's lad. Yer. The one I locked up for the night. Little fatty who cried for his ma...)* Fred feels a damp coldness cover his skin, but thankfully the policeman's beady eyes do not linger on him and his withering gaze passes onto other boys in the room. "All I'm concerned about is finding this little girl whose mother and father are worried sick."

From the tone of his voice now, Fred almost thinks the policeman seems compassionate. Even human. But he knows that can't be true. What's true is he is out to get the criminal. And the criminal is him.

Job done, the copper puts his helmet back under his arm, stands to attention, looks over at Father Mullins and nods his thanks. Father Mullins backs away and opens the classroom door for his guest. As the policeman walks to it with the innate swagger of a drum major, the boys all stand, the loud rasp of their chair legs against the floor surprising him no less than a sudden barrage of enemy gunfire. He pauses, startled.

"Thank you, Sergeant Sykes."

"Thank you, Father."

The boys feel the policeman's eyes on them long after he is gone. What Catholicism breeds in them is that they are guilty—but not, as yet, sure what they are guilty of. But there is plenty of time for that. Possibly the rest of their lives.

*

The bell rings. The lesson changes. The young priest leaves and a noisy hiatus ensues before the next teacher arrives. In the clatter of desk lids and the thump of textbooks Fred shuffles to the window and looks down.

He watches the policeman striding to the school gates. Shiny boots, measured step, arms swinging as if crossing a parade ground. The figure stops and turns, pulling the huge gates closed after him, momentarily the other side of its iron bars. Pausing...

Fred backs sharply away from the glass, fearing the brute might suddenly look up and detect him.

He doesn't look back out again. But for a good few minutes, perhaps longer, wonders if the sergeant is down there, looking up at him, knowing he did it. Just wanting proof. Just wanting to catch him, red-handed. Get a confession. Beat it out of him. Standing there all day, if he has to.

*

He sits on the filthy floorboards in the abandoned house feeling abandoned himself, knees under chin, arms wrapped round his legs, one sock up and one at half mast, school satchel dumped beside him. He has sat in silence for so long now he forgets, looking at the door of the broom cupboard. No sound has come from inside since he got there, and that frightens him. He thinks of calling out her name but doesn't. He has a good mind to go home and forget about her. Then how would she like it? Is she playing silly beggars or is she...

Perhaps she's...

He walks to the door and makes scratching noises on it with the fingernails of one hand. He can hear her moving about inside now. Panting, agitated, bleating.

"Do you like mice?" he says. "It's full of mice in there." He gets the desired result. She shrieks loudly as well as panting hard in between times. But it very quickly gets on his nerves. "Shut up! Shut your racket! You sound like a girl."

"I *am* a girl!"

"Well stop *sounding* like one!"

He doesn't know if she is obeying him but she goes quiet, completely quiet, like before. Then he can hear her sobbing, pitifully.

He doesn't like it. It sounds too much like he sounds. He's got better things to do than to listen to that. That's no fun at all. He backs away from the door and hauls up his satchel onto his shoulder.

"My brothers will get you," her voice says.

"You haven't got any brothers."

"I have. Two of them. And they're big. Bigger than you. They're grown-ups. They'll kill you."

"I don't believe you."

"One's a tanner and a prize fighter and one runs a factory and lives in Greenwich." She pronounces it as it is spelled: *Green Witch*.

"You don't even say it like that. You pronounce it 'Grennidge'."

"I don't care."

"You do care because you're lying. It's 'Grennidge', and you'd know that if your brother lived there."

"Oh, you're so clever."

"I am! I *am* clever. And you're stupid."

"And I thought you were nice."

Did she? Did she really?

"That's your fault. I didn't say I was nice. I'm not nice. I'm bad. Everybody tells me I'm bad, and I am. Bad as Judas!"

He notices his voice has become like Parkhill's and he wants to go on and tell her she is bad things, but he can't, because she isn't. She isn't those things, same as he wasn't.

What is she then? Like him? Hurt? Sorry? Innocent?

His victim has gone quiet, allowing him his musings. Then the voice returns, small, plaintive. Like another person's. Like a trapped angel. Like a butterfly in a jam jar...

"Will you let me out please?"

"No."

"I didn't do anything wrong. What did I do?"

"You had nasty thoughts. Evil thoughts. Thoughts about boys." He presses his face to the broom cupboard door. "That you liked them and wanted them to kiss you. You wanted to touch them. And, and—

and—*them* touch *you*!" He lets her think about that. Yes. Consider her misdeeds, yes—consider them well. All night if she has to. In the dark. Like *he* had to.

"Is that what *you* want?"

"What?"

"To be touched?" The whisper comes through the wood. "To be kissed?"

"No."

How close are her lips? Inches? He pulls back again. Afraid. But of what?

"Because I will if you want to." Her words seep with allure.

He cannot see her, but he can. In his mind's eye. In his camera mind she's as clear as Cleopatra on the big screen. In his big screen mind she's a star. She's voluptuous, whatever 'voluptuous' means, *"I'll let you if you want to."* she says, the lost treasure of a promise. "Are you there? Fred? Fred? *Fred?"*

"Yes."

"Don't go," she says. *"Because I'm doing it now."*

He's puzzled. He's scared. He's excited. It's a mystery. The biggest, best mystery going. But the suspense is killing him.

"What? What are you doing?"

He thinks of old scrotum-face, and sin. Of the man under the street light.

"Just open the door and see."

He laughs. "That's the oldest trick in the book. I'm not falling for that one." Then he swallows. "See what?"

He stares at the door with its scratched and peeling paint. Picturing what may be behind it. Asking himself if the reality can ever, ever be as good as the pictures. Stepping slowly closer...

"I'm lifting my skirt," says angel, butterfly, sunlight. *"I'm showing you."*

"Showing me what?"

"Showing you... All... I've... Got..."

Chubby fingers trembling, Fred reaches towards the rusty bolt. Knowing it will open the door to Salvation or Paradise or the confessional, or terror, or Hell, or the pit of endless prison, or the thrilling swirl of the Zoetrope. The organ ascends, its bass notes throbbing in his small chest with ghastly but blissful anticipation.

"Just open the door and you can see. See everything."

But his fingers never touch the cold of the metal.

She waits, but in the silence she knows. The footsteps, echoing, diminishing, confirm it.

"Fred? *Fred!* I mean it! *Come back!*"

But it is no good. The small boy is already gone.

*

He sees Union Jack bunting draped across the street from side to side, as if to welcome him home. Men with brown aprons and rolled-up sleeves are up ladders hanging it, cigarettes clasped between their lips as they add much-needed colour to the scene. The old red, white and blue. He's forgotten Empire Day is imminent. Walking under ladders is bad luck. He crosses the street. He wishes he hadn't. Under resplendent flags hanging from upstairs windows, a duo of uniformed constables wearing capes and gloves are knocking on doors.

Fred knows what they're asking even though he can't hear. They're asking local residents if they can "help with their enquiries". He slows down to a walk as he passes them, trying to act normal and nonchalantly. Trying to be like an actor. Trying not to be himself. Because as himself he might give the game away. He keeps his head down, eyes on the pavement ahead. Not on them.

They don't even pause in their conversation with a barrel of a woman with a scarf knotted round her head who repeats that she don't know nuffink. He is past them and standing on the kerb to cross the road.

"Oi! Oi, you—little man!"

Fred stops, swaying slightly, but doesn't turn. Hopes it isn't him being addressed, but knows it is. It *bloody* is. He hears the crunch of the hobnail boots behind him as one of them approaches.

He turns. Too young for a moustache, this one. Chin-strap puckering his face, bisecting fat, crab-apple cheeks.

"Your shoe lace is undone."

Not that I'm a master criminal then? Not that you want to arrest me? Not that I'm guilty as charged?

Fred crouches to do them up. The young bobby puts his hands on his hips.

"You want to watch that. You'll come a cropper."

Fred stands up and, without looking the nice constable in the eyes, carries on his way, only seeing him on the periphery of his vision, shaking his head and returning to his colleague and his task.

*

Evening now, and he is kneeling on the carpet, playing with his Bing '1' gauge clockwork tin-plate model train set as his parents talk, thinking he is too absorbed in his play to be listening.

"They're searching the canal," says his father. "If they find her, he'll swing for it, whoever he is."

"Shsh! Love of God. Don't talk like that in front of him. You know he's got a vivid imagination."

Fred carries on pushing his toy locomotive round the track with the accompaniment of suitable noises, pretending he isn't paying attention. But he is. Of course he is.

"What those poor parents are going through…" says his mother, lapsing into her own general opinion on the matter. "Children are a burden, such a burden and an agony…" Fred feels his father looking down at him, perhaps not so sure the lad isn't taking it all in, and wishing he wasn't, but not about to tell his wife to curb her tongue. "Sometimes I think it's better not to grow up at all, with all the pains of existence ahead of you. Sure, happiness is an illusion—like an actor on the silver screen."

"Best say a prayer for her, then," her husband murmurs through his teeth.

"I shall," she replies, sensing a veiled slight against her character. "Oh, I shall."

"Had a feeling you would."

He stands up, folds his newspaper, and heads for the living room.

"Where are you going?" she asks.

Fred's father stops, holding back a sigh.

"You get out there and help them search, Bill Hitchcock." She is firm, as sometimes she can be. Nothing if not unpredictable. "I want you out there, where everyone can see you. And I want you to be the last one who comes home, d'you hear me?"

*

The black surface of the water barely ripples, periodically lit by the scan of policemen's bull's-eye lamps. A search party is out. Their footsteps echo in the brick drum of the tunnel, but they exchange not a word—their ponderous and unenviable work too serious, the possible outcome too solemn, to be leavened by chit-chat. They are skirting the realm of ghosts, and in dread expectation of the unspeakable. Methodically, their time-honoured art, they look all over, in corners, bushes, inlets, behind discarded crates and rubbish, dirt behind ears, secrets in pockets, bending over half-broken fences, shining the beams up at the curved underside of the canal bridge.

Sergeant Sykes with his Kitchener moustache is one of their number. He moves along the tow path with a long bargee's pole delving into the water, looking for anything that might be lodged, submerged... Anything, or anyone... With what may be misconstrued as some kind of macabre relish he moves his pole in a regular motion as he walks, like a ferryman with an oar.

Further along the tow path Fred's father, Bill, walks into view from a pathway leading to the lock gates, two men at his side—the thin-necked assistants from the shop. Grocery boys, out of their overalls. Should be in the pub. Will be, at the end of this. Whatever the outcome. Quick snifter. Brass monkeys, what it is. Still, got to be done…

The policeman watches Bill as Bill speaks to them, sending them off in two different directions, to the sluices and the sewer-pipe. Without given instruction, Fred's father has a broom handle and starts using it to prod at the canal-side foliage, hooking aside the spiky remains of a bicycle wheel.

Taking a breather, he notices the policeman still looking at him. He looks back at the man. Does not hesitate in doing so. Does not shift in any way or even blink.

The policeman stares also, in no hurry to desist from this, but the stare demands nothing—no answer, no acknowledgement. It is confident and knowing and empty, but will not back down. But of what does it constitute? Surliness? Pity? Threat?

Fred's father notices that one of his own shirtsleeves has rolled down to his wrist. He wipes his hand on his waistcoat and rolls it back up. His bare arms are dirty and there are smudges on his face. He wears no collar. He has no stud.

The policeman cricks his neck over his shoulder and whispers to the officer next to him. They exchange a small, unpleasant laugh.

Fred's father knows the remark was about him in some way and whatever its contents, he doesn't like it. He wants to get away. He wants to go home. But he can't go home. He has to be here.

The policeman lowers to a crouch, leaning on his pole which is in the water.

As he stares into it his face, lit by the bulldog lamp at his feet, is reflected upside-down in the murky water beneath him.

*

The bony grin of a skull and crossbones flag peers out from the cover of *Treasure Island*, lying as it does in the shadows at the foot of Fred's bed.

He tries to get to sleep, listening to his mother gently weeping in her perpetual anguish in the next room. He wishes he could go to her but he can't. He wishes he could solve the mystery but he can't. He wishes he could stop her fear, but he can't. He can't even stop his own.

But then he gets an idea how it has to end. He is good at endings. The ending is the most important part, but the most difficult. But he knows what he has to do.

*

The kitchen drawer next to the sink slides open. A brass band is playing outside. Shooting a furtive glance to the door, he takes out a carving knife and puts it in his school satchel, quickly buckling it up.

He trots down the wooden stairs with his satchel over his shoulder. The dingy back room is empty. He walks through the darkness of the shop to the front door. His father is at the cash register serving a customer. For Empire Day he is dressed in the khaki twill service dress uniform of the British army, with puttees and a wide-brimmed tropical hat pinned up on one side. Fred doesn't know whether his father fought in the war in South Africa or if he killed people. The idea of it is strange. If he ever did he has kept silent on the matter—as he is on every matter. He does not explain his costume and Fred does not ask.

While upstairs, his mother enters the kitchen and picks up her knitting. She sees that the cutlery drawer is open, and walks over and shuts it.

*

The brass band music is jolly, but distant. Bird song replaces it. Not unpleasant. He passes the spot where he and the other boys tried to squash the mouse with their bricks. He goes to the dark inside. Straight to the door to the broom cupboard.

He can hear nothing within. He puts his ear to it.

Still nothing. He wonders if she is dead. Already. He wonders if he is too late.

He kneels down and un-buckles his satchel. He takes out the carving knife. He delves back inside and takes out something wrapped in a handkerchief.

It is a piece of his mother's fruit cake.

He places it down on the floorboards. He cuts it in two with the carving knife.

He wraps one slice in the handkerchief.

He pushes it through the gap under the door. It barely fits. He prods it. It disappears into the gloom.

He crabs away a few yards, leaving a trail in the thick snow of dust.

The carving knife still gripped tightly, he eats the other piece of fruit cake with his free hand. Licking his fingers one by one when they get too sticky.

"Cherries," a voice says. "I don't like cherries."

"Pick them out then."

"I won't pick them out. I'll spit them out."

Fred watches the darkness in the gap under the door as the girl moves around inside.

"Are you still crying?" he asks.

"Why do you care?"

"Do you like the cake?"

"No."

Fred finishes his own portion regardless.

"You won't really tell them, will you? Your brothers?" No answer was the stern reply. "It was just a game. We were just playing." No answer, a second time. "Don't say it was me. Say it was an accident. Say it was a tramp." Still no answer. Fred stands up. His legs feel wobbly. "I'll let you out, but you've got to promise you won't say it was me. Not to anybody." The girl still hasn't said a word. "…Hello?"

"Hello."

"Well?"

"Well what?"

"Will you do what I say if I set you free?"

"Yes."

"Do you promise?"

"Yes. Yes."

"On your mother and father's lives? Cross your heart and hope to die?"

"Yes."

Fred takes a step forward, gives the bolt a good wiggle and pulls it back. He retreats quickly, nervously—pulling the door open at the same time. A pigeon, trapped and now free, flies into his face, hooting. He paws away its fluttering wings, shutter-like, and button eyes.

Behind it she skitters, The Girl With Yellow Hair, semi-huddled in what used to be the dark. But what strikes him first is that her hair isn't yellow any more. It is lank with grime and cobwebs and pigeon white, no longer brushed and neat and glowing—nothing about her *glows*. She is not dignified or smart or clean but dishevelled, damp, her ankle-length skirt pulled up and torn and stained with droppings. This isn't the pretty girl he met in the street. This one is *dirty*. ("Needs a good bar of carbolic," as his mother might say.) This one looks *poor*. Worst of all she has a cut over one eye, swollen like a boxer's, with lines of dried blood down her cheek. What kind of girl looks like a boy after a fight? Is a girl with blood on her face and fear in her eyes easier or harder to fall in love with? And is it easier or harder for her to fall in love with you?

The girl gets stumblingly to her feet and emerges quickly. So quickly he has to side step to get out of her way. But she loses her balance and has to prop herself against a crusted, peeling wall.

Her transformation shocks him. Did he do this? No... This isn't what was supposed to happen. This wasn't the plan...

She stands with her back to him, chest heaving.

"I didn't mean anything," he says near tears. "I thought it was a joke."

She doesn't turn.

She gasps. Chokes. Splutters. Sobs catching in her throat.

"Now you know what it's like," he says, almost sobbing too.

"What *what's* like?"

He says: "Being afraid."

Without turning, his girl hurries stiffly out into sunshine, breaking into an inelegant, lolloping run as she gets to the garden.

To his own surprise, Fred stays inside the derelict room, not moving from the spot, the carving knife held flat across his chest. He hears the pigeons, more of them, upstairs. Filling the room. Fluttering and scratching. Fighting something. Attacking. He doesn't like to imagine what's happening up there because it sounds like there are millions, and they are getting louder and louder in his head.

*

They are looking straight at us, frozen in time. William Hitchcock, still in the khaki uniform, standing in an upright pose holding the bridle of his horse, Fred sitting in the saddle dressed in a child's version of the same. We can see nothing of the little boy's fears or dreams as he sits gazing into the lens. The shop window is the backdrop, all its wares on display, onion strings and hares hung up by their feet—an advertising opportunity never to be passed up, as Mrs Hitchcock tells him. Father and son hold their poses as the photographer exposes the plate, then packs up his tripod and moves on, doffing his cap.

Bill knows that in the dark of the window behind him, his wife Em sits, far away from the celebrations of the common people. Leaving life for her husband and son to report in despatches from the front.

*

The children have a day off for it. Rule Britannia and whatnot. But then it's back to normal. No strawberry jelly or trifle, or pigeon pie and mash like mountains making trestle tables groan. Now it is Fred dressed in a sports vest and baggy shorts at the boundary as his schoolfriends play cricket. He has lost interest in the game as he always does. Mind in a far off land. In crime and punishment. The breathless chase. The runaway train. The police in relentless pursuit. The pitiless rogue and his victim, the woman in peril, a hair's breadth from violent death...

She screams, in his mind—but what he hears is his name, and snaps out of his daydream.

A black flapping shape like a tumbling crow stands at the crease, a gangly young priest having called the match to a halt. A ball bounces, caught by the wicket-keeper at the stumps. The rest of the players stand inert, and curious, all eyes on Fred. He is beckoned furiously.

Fred points at himself—*me?*

The spindly rake of a priest beckons harder, grim-faced. Fiercely impatient now. *Yes, you, boy! You!*

Oh no. Oh damn. Oh Hell.

Fred has no choice but to hurry to him briskly or face a box round the ears, but a box round the ears might be the least of his worries. What if... what if they—*know?*

The crow-shaped man leads him away from the cricket pitch, one hand gripping his shoulder so tight it hurts, but Fred dare not blubber or he knows he will get something that hurts much more. If he travels any faster his feet will leave the ground and he doesn't like it. And he doesn't like not knowing what is coming either. But he *does* know. He *does* know for certain—but he's praying, praying inside more desperately than he's ever done in his short life, that he's wrong.

They reach the school building without a word. He's escorted towards a familiar door, the huge hand still firmly attached to his shoulder, cutting off the blood, making him lean to one side, almost buckling under it.

The door looms. The crow priest knocks.

Fred wonders what it must feel like to walk to the scaffold. To feel the weight of manacles on your wrists. To hear the judge at the Old Bailey with that little black cap on his head say that you will be *taken from this place and be hung by the neck until you are dead.* He wonders if you feel this kind of hand on your shoulder, if you've cut up your missus, if you've robbed a bank, if you've plotted to overthrow the King, if you've kissed—

"Enter."

The door yawns. Fred steps inside. The young priest doesn't follow.

Father Mullins sits behind his desk, fingertips forming a steeple. To one side of him stands Sister Maureen Quinn, a nun with a face that would pickle an egg. But worse than that—*much* worse than that—is that in front of the desk with her back to Fred stands the girl, Olga Butterworth, her hands obediently behind her back and her head slightly bowed.

God! Oh God!

Fred wants to run. Or at least beat on the door to be let out.

Please! Please!

But that would be giving the game away, he knows that. And the one thing he can't do is Give The Game Away...

"And you've said none of this to the Sergeant?"

Olga shakes her head. She glances over her shoulder at Fred, detecting in the old man's eyes that someone has entered. Fred blinks hard. That the nasty cut on her eye now has a bandage over it.

She's blind. Blind!

His stomach turns over.

"Hitchcock," continues Father Mullins. "Come in and stand next to this young lady. I have some questions I want to ask you."

His innards protesting, Fred steps forward and halts slightly behind but alongside the girl. He takes care that she can't easily look sideways at him. He doesn't want her to. He stares at his shoelaces.

"Look up."

For the first time, he sees a stuffed bird in a display case in the corner of the room. He thinks it is a cormorant. It has a fish in its mouth. He wonders where the taxidermists get the eyes because a real eye would decay. It can't be a real eye.

"Look at *me*, boy. Do you know the empty house behind the allotments?"

Fred snaps his neck erect. "Yes, Father."

"Have you ever been there?"

The slightest hesitation. "Yes, Father. Sometimes I play there with my friends."

"What friends, exactly?"

"Parkhill. Murphy. O'Connor, Father."

"Did you take Olga there?"

"No, Father."

"Are you sure about that?"

"Yes, Father."

The chair creaks. So does the man. "Then why do you think she said you did?"

Fred begs all that is holy that his cheeks aren't flushing. He hates his cheeks. "I—I don't know, sir. She, she must have been mistaken."

"Mistaken? How?"

"It must've been someone else who took her there."

"You mean she got it wrong?"

Fred nods.

"You mean it was a case of mistaken identity?"

"Yes, Father."

"Somebody of your height, weight, build...?"

Realising the ridiculousness of that idea, Fred accurately senses the scepticism behind the priest's words. And sees that sideways glance to the nun.

"No, Father."

"Who, then?"

He tries not to stumble. "Somebody—someone not like me at all, sir. Probably."

Mullins leans forward, easing his dark weight onto his elbows, flattened hands under his chin, eyes shining and cold, like those of the cormorant in the display case.

"Then why would she say it was you, pray?"

The boy's mind grasps at feathers in the air. "Because she wants to get me into trouble, Father."

"Why would she do that?"

His thoughts tumble. "Because she doesn't like me."

"Why doesn't she like you?"

The words cascade before he can even think about them or snatch them back. "I—I don't know, sir. Because I'm fat. Because I frightened her once. In the street. She called me a big fat baby."

The air in the room shifts as Olga flinches at the lie. He sees this and hears an intake of breath. He thinks she will speak up and denounce him, but she doesn't. Father Mullins sees her reaction, though, he's sure.

"So let me get this straight." Mullins drags his rheumy eyes to the face of the girl in front of him, then back to the boy at her side. "You didn't see her on the day she disappeared. You didn't talk about going to the pictures..."

"Yes I did, sir. But we didn't go because she didn't want to. So I went home and she..." He doesn't want his lies to become so elaborate that he becomes unstuck. That's the last thing he wants. "...she went somewhere else."

"You didn't go to the house together?"

"No, sir. Father."

"So she's a liar?"

Softly. "Yes, Father."

"Speak up."

"Yes, Father."

Mullins removes his glasses and rubs his eyes. The folds of wrinkled skin bulge and line round his fingertips. The impassive nun's hands are hidden in her voluminous sleeves. Fred half expects that she has a whip up there in case of emergencies. Or a meat cleaver. He wonders if she has ears under the wimple that encloses her vinegary visage at all, or if they've been sliced off, accounting for her acid demeanour.

Then he has an idea. An idea better than any story idea he dreams up at night time, or any idea for motion pictures he wants to see in the local flea-pit. This is a humdinger and he is keen to fill the silence with it:

"And I did see her with a man once. A grown-up. And it wasn't her father because I know what her father looks like."

"That's not—!"

"Silence, child!" Galvanised, Sister Maureen launches from behind the desk and is standing over Olga, teeth bared, a tree shaken by a storm, branches near to snapping. Olga recoils, jutting towards Fred, raising a protective arm—fearing the fierce blow of a hand, or worse.

"Miss Butterworth!" The voice of Father Mullins freezes them both. "You've had your say. This is Master Hitchcock's chance to defend himself against these—these *vile* allegations."

Allegations?

Fred no longer knows what to think. Is he accused or is he not accused?

Allegations?

He expected an assumption of guilt. He thinks of the policeman peering through the peep hole and gets the rank whiff of urine in his nostrils.

Guilty, Sonny Jim!

All the evidence is stacked against him, and the girl broke her promise not to tell. She betrayed him. Yer. He was silly to trust her. He hears the policeman telling him that. He was stupid to think she was nice. She was nasty. Horrid. She was destined for Hell. Didn't he tell her that, just as he was told it when *he* was imprisoned? So she *deserves* to get the blame. It's her fault after all. All of it. He wouldn't even *be here* if not for *her*, would he?

He realises old Mullins is staring through him. In his tool box of stares, it is the one he uses most frequently, and to greatest effect. Fred chooses to stare back at him, trying to match the coldness he sees. Unblinking. Unfeeling. Intimidating. Powerful. Truthful. Right. Is this the way things are done? Is this the way you get your way? Is this how grown-ups get away with things, he wonders? *The one who blinks first, loses*. He will have to remember that, long after the playground. *Stare, and never look away. Never show you are afraid. Ever. Ever. Ever.* Never show what you are thinking. Not *really* thinking. Or feeling.

"All right." The elderly priest's patience is finite. "Let's get to the bottom of this before Sergeant Sykes arrives." Fred shivers and sees the peep-hole rasp shut. Hears the footsteps echo in the wet chill of the cell. Feels his willy go cold as ice. "Is that the sum total of why she doesn't like you?"

Fred thinks on his feet. "N-no, sir." He is not sure he has them yet. He has the hook in their mouths but he doesn't know yet if he can reel them in. It will be down to how he tells it. The story. It is all in the telling.

"I don't like to say in front of..."

"Say it."

The sharpness of the syllables, like a blade, frightens him. The old Jesuit's exasperation is palpable.

"Come along. Come along. Your academic future is at stake here, boy. Not to mention the reputation of this school."

Fred gulps and looks furtively at the nun, who looks no less artificial than the painted statues at the altar in the chapel, then looks away from them both. Making the most of the flush that has come to his face now. Wanting it to come because it will convince them he is embarrassed. And convincing him is all he wants.

"She... she wanted to show me her—" He swallows. "...private parts, sir, Father. And, and I said I didn't want to see them. And..."

"Horrid creature," says Sister Maureen.

"Wait a minute, wait a minute..." Father Mullins closes his eyes, holds up a hand. "Alfred, listen to me very carefully. This is extremely serious. You are absolutely sure you had nothing to do with Olga going missing? Not in the slightest? Even by accident? You didn't do anything bad?"

"Bad?" Bafflement. He'd learnt from the best actors of the silver screen. "What could I do bad, sir? I'm only a little boy."

Mullins leans back in his large chair, seeming in some degree of pain and anguish as he does so. He picks up a pencil and taps it on his desk nervously, one end then the other—peering at Olga as he does so. Tongue pressing into his cheek.

"She has lied before, Father," says Sister Maureen. "Several times."

"Has she indeed?"

"And stolen from other girls. Oh yes."

This is news to Fred. But welcome news, he has to admit. He risks darting his eyes sideways, the merest flicker.

Olga's expression is one of sullen defiance.

"Well," says the priest, arranging his papers. "We don't want to waste time with fantasies of an imaginative little girl and her foolish pranks, designed to get diligent, hard working schoolboys blamed for things they didn't do." The writing implement jabs the air repeatedly. "You will not repeat this balderdash, young lady. Not to Sergeant Sykes, and not to your mother and father, do you hear me?"

Fred cannot breathe. Dare not.

The pencil drops to the blotter, rolls. A sudden thought. "*Have* you said this to your mother and father?"

"Answer!" Sister Maureen yelps shrilly, clipping Olga Butterworth on the back on the head. Fred almost feels it himself, and jerks. He averts his gaze, looking at the floor. He sees Olga's scuffed boots. Grubby hem.

"No, Father."

"What *have* you said?"

"I told them I didn't remember, Father," she says.

"Another lie," Sister Maureen decrees.

Olga looks no less sullen. No less defiant. Fred expects her to look cowed and scared, but she isn't. Not a bit. Not even a tiny bit.

"You reserved your concoction for us," says Father Mullins. "Well…"

Olga says nothing.

"I suggest that you tell your parents the truth." The paperwork on his desk cannot bear any more rearranging. "That you went exploring in that empty house like the silly girl you are, to look for toys and whatnot.

You clambered inside that cupboard and inadvertently the door closed and locked itself behind you. That's what happened, isn't it?"

The nun raises her hand in preparation for another blow.

"Yes, Father," says the girl, without recoiling this time.

"Good." Mullins gives Fred a long look, then directs it at Olga with a deep and abiding superiority in every way conceivable: physical, verbal, legal, moral, spiritual. Especially spiritual. "You should know that only when you confess your sins can you be truly forgiven. In order to be free, you must first acknowledge your guilt. Do you acknowledge your guilt?"

Without pause Olga says, "Yes, Father." As if in automatic reply to the most innocuous of questions in the classroom. As if it didn't even matter any more what she said. And perhaps it didn't.

"Good. Do you have anything more to tell us?"

"No, Father."

Mullins looks at the nun and nods. Sister Maureen shakes her capacious sleeves and escorts Olga to the door.

"You'll be punished for this, you little madam!" Fred hears the woman say (if nuns counted themselves as women: he wasn't sure about that). "Showing us all up like this! Who do you think you are? Never speak of it again—not a word, do you hear me? Not a *word!*"

"Sister Maureen?" The priest rubbed the plough-lines of his forehead. "Will you tell Sergeant Sykes that we've explained the mystery, or shall I?"

"I will, Father."

He nods. "Very well."

The door closes. The nun and the schoolgirl have gone.

Fred stands there, eager to be dismissed himself. But bollock-features stares at him for a little while, perhaps hoping that the boy's inexpressive gaze will break into an emotion of some kind. It doesn't. Peculiar lad. Bright enough. But something... Fred shuffles his feet. For a few moments Mullins considers the significance of this: the significance of everything. Good. Evil. The machinations of a small child's mind, and soul. The perplexity of it. Where it begins and ends. Then decides to leave God to be the knower of such things, and us to master only the errors of the flesh. He turns to a mundane pile of essays that require marking, and gives a dismissive if theatrical wave of the hand.

"Alfred?"

Fred stops and turns, with one hand on the door handle.

"Father?"

He hasn't seen this look in the old man's eyes before. "Find kindness in your life."

*

Fred shuts the study door after him. He looks down the corridor and sees Sister Maureen Quinn and Olga walking past the cloakroom towards the dull light of the playground. The girl, though tall, has her shoulders hunched, head down. Her woolly sleeves cover her hands. The nun dwarfs her. *Who is on their way to the scaffold now?*

He smiles. Almost.

He wonders what punishment she is in for. How many Hail Marys or worse. Not that he can do anything about it—why should he? She didn't care about him, did she? Why should *he* care about *her*?

He imagines a title-card on a movie screen: "The End". A so-and-so production. But a shadow steps into view, blocking out the struggling rays of the sun filtered through the glazing of the creaky swing doors. A figure that makes his pulse race and his head pound. The policeman stands at the far end of the corridor and Sister Maureen stops and talks to him, the girl's small wrist harshly in her talon grip. She talks a lot, and Sergeant Sykes listens, occasionally nodding. He takes out his small notebook and licks the tip of his pencil.

Fred wishes he could see his face, but is also thankful he can't. He knows what the man is being told, of course, but sees nothing in his posture to tell him whether he takes it at face value or not. Whether the case is closed or he has his suspicions. Suspicions about what? Whom? He'd swear the copper is deliberately giving nothing away—

just standing there with his snake-clip belt tight across his stomach with his legs planted firmly apart.

Chin on her chest, Olga Butterworth stands there without speaking or moving.

The policeman turns his head. Catches sight of Fred, watching.

The hand bell is still ringing. Schoolboys pour out of a nearby classroom, filling the corridor in a gushing torrent, and Fred is gratefully lost in the stream.

*

Polished black boots step over discarded bricks, ferns, foliage, cracks in the paving. The leather of them squeaks. The policeman, Sergeant Stanley Sykes of this parish, chin-strap tight, walks into the debris-strewn room, his weight crunching nuggets of plaster, snapping strips of lath. Birds coo and flutter in the attic, the broken roof giving them access, open as it is to the heavens. Mating and meandering.

Scratching the match-board of his cheek, he walks over to the broom cupboard in question. Footsteps left in the white dust.

The door is almost shut, but not quite. He pulls it open and closed—as if trying out how this "door" thing works. A simian new to civilisation and its fancy trickery.

He bangs it, shuts the rusty bolt, then tugs it open again horizontally. Orange flakes pepper his hands. He claps them off, brushes his trouser legs.

He looks at the small space inside—grubby, chipped paint, pigeon droppings. Smelling of human excrement too. Piss. Shit. Little wonder. Poor bloody thing. How long? Not the least of his questions...

He sees something on the floor. He plucks at his knees and crouches down. His boots sigh. Well, well. He puts on black gloves before picking it up. As he pokes the valleys between his leather fingers, he smiles. The smile couldn't grow wider if he'd found a treasure trove. Which, now he thinks about it, he has.

*

The halo of a paraffin lamp descends the wooden stairs, filling the back room with a ruddy, imperfect glow. Fred's father holds it at chest height. If he was undressed he has dressed swiftly—shirt unbuttoned, slippers on, pulling the elastic of his braces onto his shoulders. The knuckle-knock sounds a second time, well-practised and formal in its musicality. Three raps followed by two.

He walks through his shop to the front door accompanied by the tunnel of light. Getting closer he can see the distinctive silhouette of a policeman through the rain-dotted glass. He draws the bolt top and bottom and unlocks the Chubb. The lamp illuminates the waxy pallor of his friend from the police station. If he can call him a friend. He doubts whether he can any more.

"You'd better come with me."

There's a smugness and satisfaction about the man's expression that Fred's father wants to defy. But he will not defy the law. His wife would never forgive it. He has to behave. That's what she always wants, for her husband to behave. His lips tighten to a line.

The policeman is not waiting for a discussion on the matter.

"Bill?"

Fred's father looks over his shoulder. Fred's mother has descended in the dark to the back room. Even without seeing her face he can tell from the rise and fall of her shoulders and the tension in her body she is anxious.

"Your wife too, please," says the policeman.

Fred's father back walks to his wife, her hand being extended for him to take, else she might float away or collapse—any manner of horrors.

"Shall I shout up to the boy?"

The woman shakes her head. "The boy's asleep."

Her husband fetches her hat, her white cotton gloves, her fox fur stole. Helps her don it, like protection. Then puts on his own hat and scarf. He asks no questions, as he can tell the policeman will tell them what he wants, when he wants, and not before.

*

An unholy hubbub exudes from the Public Bar. The policeman sits with Bill and Em at one of the small round tables in the Saloon. More civilised there. Less *unrestrained*. For the lady. He has a pint in front of him but the others have no glasses in front of them. No wish to drink. To socialise. Only to listen.

Licking the ale froth from his upper lip and moustache, the policeman takes out something from his pocket and places it on the table between them.

He carefully unwraps it.

It is a slice of fruit cake in a grubby handkerchief.

They look at it. Then they look at him.

The policeman says nothing as he raises his glass and tilts back his head. Savouring the moment no less than he savours the hops.

Husband and wife stare down at the evidence. Evidence of what? What is he trying to say? Why isn't he saying anything?

But the policeman is in no hurry for them to grasp all it implies. He has all the time in the world. He is enjoying this. Enjoying it immensely. It's an unparalleled pleasure to him and he wants to extend its life indefinitely.

He downs the rest of the pint slowly but in one draft, placing the empty glass back down on the table. A random pattern of white foam slides slowly down the sides of it, pooling at the bottom.

They recognise the fruit cake.

They recognise the handkerchief.

Of course they do.

Fred's mother looks drained. Helpless. Made of glass. Her smallness, her delicacy, her fragility, make her attractive. She is snappable, breakable, so easily. Some men are attracted to that. Some men think they can mend women. Make it better. Then there are *other* men…

The policeman knows what he wants. It is obvious what he wants. He doesn't need to put it in words. He likes the idea that they find the words all on their own. That's much more to his liking, that is. He is looking directly at the petite woman, trying to engage her eye as he runs his index finger round the rim of his pint glass, then strokes the froth off it onto his tongue.

He takes out a packet of Will's Gold Flake. Opens it. Slides one out half-way and offers it to her.

She doesn't respond. Doesn't even look. If he'd shown her part of his anatomy she couldn't be more rigid, or feel more abused.

With indifference to her reaction, he takes the cigarette out of the pack and puts one end to her lips. She refuses to part them. He inserts it just the same. Her eyes flicker and her dry lips open as he pushes the cigarette between them.

She doesn't move as he holds it there a little too long. Daring the man of the household to react—if he *is* a man. And if he *does* react, what? Only a bit of fun, mate! Only a bit of harmless fun. What's wrong wi' you?

Smiling as if to put her at ease, but not that at all, the policeman slides his fingers down the length of it. He strikes a Lucifer briskly against the sandpaper of a matchbox and lights the tip, still grinning. He could light it on the fire burning inside Fred's father and he knows it, but he's not hugely bothered. He loves that fact. Loves seeing people squirm. Loves them not being able to act, for fear of his badge and position. Why wouldn't he, eh? One of the perks of the job, innit... Like the moral instruction of minors, in exchange for a turnip or two. I scratch your back, you scratch mine, cock. That's the East End, my son. That's proper London, that is.

I scratch your back. You scratch mine.

Taking another Gold Flake from the packet with his own lips, he lights that from the same match, puffing smoke into the air from the corner of his mouth before blowing it out. He drops the blackened, curled stick of wood into the ash tray.

Bill Hitchcock is not stupid. He knows what is going on here. The wordless bargain that is being made while the animal breath laughs and the tankards clink next door, and the beer fug seeps through, stale as a workman's sweat in the air. He is sickened by the thought of it. Sickened to his soul. But he's damned if he knows a way out of it. He doesn't. He fails. He is a failure, which is perhaps what he was always destined to be.

He stares at the slice of fruit cake.

The policeman shrugs, mainly with his eyebrows—as if to say, with the merest effort: *Up to you, mate.*

Before her husband can do anything, and he wants to, Emma Jane is standing and her husband is startled to see her glide round the table to stand beside the policeman's chair. She grips her handbag in tight fingers. Chin set. Eyes fixed. Shoulders back. It's clear from her expression she wants to leave now, but not with her husband—with *him.*

Fred's father sits aghast, the fight gone out of him before any fight was begun. Already the day, this scene, is etching itself into him. Carving into him until it draws blood. And he is grey and defeated, still keeping his emotions in check for her sake. For *her* sake? It's madness and he wants to scream it, but will it even move the air if he does, will it stop the wheel that turns?

She pretends she cannot see the furnace of his anger under the surface and gently shakes her head. He's not to think of her. This is her decision. It's the only way, and they both know it.

Jaw clenched, Bill stands up sharply.

He glares at the policeman, the look on his face telling him he knows what the man is doing and will never forgive him for it. But he has no choice.

Fred's mother picks up the piece of fruit cake, the tiny pressure releasing its smell and taking her back to the kitchen on the day she made it. Her nostrils quiver. She folds the handkerchief neatly over it and places it in her husband's hand, closing his fingers around it. He can do nothing, but he can leave, and he does.

Left alone, she fights back tears, but is beguiled and enamoured of the inner voice that tells her she is strong. She wishes that voice had spoken up before now. She would like to have heard it more often.

The policeman drills out his cigarette in the ashtray and stands, straightening his tunic. He crooks his elbow like a bridegroom, asking her to take his arm. Even now, knowing the hideousness which is to come, she takes it as the respectable gesture it is. It serves her not to believe it a sham.

He pats the gloved hand on his forearm and escorts her to the door to the smoke and stench of the Public Bar. To the swamp. To the mire. To Hell. It takes her, and she's greeted with laughter and applause, no better or worse than a woman of the night, and the door swings shut after her. Through the semi-opaque glass their shapes merge with the crowd – fangs and pitchforks; the martyr and the Philistines; bears, hyenas, gazelles; the predators and the prey.

*

Fred's father wonders if she is calling out for him. He prefers to believe she is not. But he wants to call her. Her name. Just say it. Just shout it. Instead he stares into the water, hearing nothing on the night air but trains. He thinks of his son's obsession—timetables, bus routes, the picture house. Fred. Son... Dear God in Heaven...

He looks into his hand which holds the handkerchief and its contents.

He pulls back his arm and throws it with a pugilist's welt into the canal. It almost takes him off his feet, and every ounce of breath out of him in a grunt.

When he looks he sees only the moon reflected in rippling slivers. Nothing in the centre of the widening rings. Nothing at all.

*

Footsteps echo. Shoe leather squeals. The policeman has the big ring of keys in his hand. He unlocks the cell door.

Fred's mother enters.

The policeman comes in behind her. He doesn't shut the door heavily, but even closing it gently results in the inevitable clang. The sound bounces off the brickwork. Echoes through the corridors. Pierces her. Chills her marrow. The smell is inconceivable. The surfaces hard. She sees no softness, no frills. Nothing she would call homely, or feminine. No vestige of human comfort. Nothing of <u>her</u> home, <u>her</u> life.

What did she expect? Not tenderness. Not that. But...

She hears the pop, pop, pop as he unbuttons his police tunic.

Without turning, she uncoils her fur wrap and places it down on the bench, crouching slightly with her knees together. On top of it she carefully places her hat and her earrings. They gleam. She wants to remember how they gleam.

He takes her hand and unbuttons the wrist of her white cotton glove, slipping it off finger by finger, tugging the last as it comes away. He performs the same ritual on the other.

He slips his thumbs under his braces and lifts them off one shoulder then the other. He unfastens and unbuttons his trousers.

She thinks of the butchery in her husband's shop and wants to vomit. The redness and flesh. The dead eyes. The hanging limbs of bird and beast. The tufts of grey-speckled fur. The tightened skin over muscle. The taut shine of liver before it is seared in the pan.

Soon she is naked.

Soon it begins.

Her white palms and knees rub into the filth of the walls and floor. Fingernails claw at her back, the rancid blanket stuffing her mouth, teeth and beer breath gnawing her cheek, a spike breaking into her.

Soon it begins, and never ends.

*

She faces the wall, eyes open. She can hear customers downstairs in the shop. They trill happily, exchanging the time of day and chuckling with the staff, but it cannot warm her skin. Mrs Bates with her bosom, Mr Jarvis with his gammy leg. She hears the cash register ting. She can even see the sunlight trying to get through the drawn curtains, seeping round the edges. Urging her, but she doesn't want to be urged.

She is curled up under the sheets with both hands squeezed between her thighs. She cannot separate them.

Her husband—a good man, and rare—enters with a tray. He places down a cup of tea on the bedside table and sits on the bed beside her.

They hear the door bang, and before they can speak—if they wanted to speak—their son bursts in excitedly, dressed in his school uniform. The sombre spell of the room vanishes instantly, as if a ray of light has broken through the clouds. Her ray of light. Her clouds.

Fred is surprised—but not completely surprised—to see his mother in bed. He wonders if he should go.

Not a bit of it. She struggles to sit up. The old ritual. His father puffs up the pillow behind her. She valiantly puts on a smile.

"What happened in school today?"

"Not much."

He's teasing her.

He removes a rubber band and unfurls a painting he has made on grey cartridge paper. He hands it to her.

Her smile widens as she sees what is in the corner.

"A gold star for Art! Will you look at this!"

She shows it to William fleetingly, then takes it back, shaking her head in proud astonishment. Tears welling up in her eyes—for reasons the boy thinks he comprehends, but does not. Can not. And will not. Because he will never know. Of that much his parents are certain.

"'An exceptional piece of work by a born artist.'" She reads the teacher's comment aloud. "'Excellent.' Oh my word... 'Excellent.' Come here."

He goes to her as he is bidden. She envelops him with hugs and showers him with a flotilla of kisses. He doesn't like it but he does, even though he wonders what a girl feels like rather than his mother. He smells perfume, or aniseed balls, but he smells something else under it he doesn't like. Something like the smell of a wet dog or the canal, or the bleach used to mop the floor. He doesn't know what.

His father digs into his waistcoat pocket and hands him a bright, shiny shilling.

"Well done, son."

Son.

Fred glows. It means everything to him.

Everything.

He'd like to see Parkhill and the others now. He'd like to see Father Mullins. He's like to see the policeman, even, in his stupid moustache and polished shoes. He'd give them all what for. He'd tell them all what he thought of them. Because nothing can hurt him now. Nothing can scare him. Not now. Not today.

*

And he thinks of it now in the dimness of his recall, that moment when he showed his mother the little gold star. Of the little man he was becoming. Maturing like a wine. The grape informed by the soil, the hillsides, the rain.

*

When the boy has left the room, his father and mother look at each other. Afraid even their eyes might harm the other. She finds her hand taken in his, so lightly, as he did on her wedding day.

*

There are many days of education ahead for their child. Many a day of the altar boy trudging off to Saint Ignatius High School for Boys in his uniform and cap, heavy satchel over his shoulder. To work. To learn. To be praised. To be cowed. To be made.

On this morning, wrapped in his thoughts as ever, he chances to look up and see Olga Butterworth walking along on the pavement opposite, parallel to him, to the Convent School adjacent to his. He hasn't seen her for days. Not since he was in Father Mullins' study. He'd supposed she was being kept at home, or had moved away, or was ill. He thought himself a detective, but there you are: he wasn't a very good one.

Olga stops, and turns. She watches him, but he does not break his stride. He has seen her expression. She has no expression. Just a scar on her cheek bone and her eye is still swollen and bloodshot. She is not blind. She can see. She can look, and she is looking at him.

He pretends he hasn't noticed.

He walks.

As he nears the school gates he hears the sound of his friends in the playground, arguing, joshing, joking, punching.

He trails his hand along the wrought iron railings.

Looks through the bars at them, gripping two either side of his face. The applause rises until it becomes deafening. A roar.

*

Ladies and gentlemen… He has thrilled us. He has scared us. He has given us excitement, tension, romance and terror like no other director who shouted "Action!"… Please welcome the beneficiary of the American Film Institute's Life Achievement Award. The "Master of Suspense"…

*

The whole room rises to their feet at the mention of his name. The swell of it washes over him. He is drowned in it, and touched by it and overpowered by it—all the time, simultaneously pondering what it means.

What is he doing here? The ballroom of the Beverly Hilton Hotel—

March 7th, 1979. Basking in the never-ending applause from dozens of tables populated by the Hollywood great and good, dressed to the nines. Furs his late mother could only ever dream of. Tuxedos a million miles—and literally thousands of miles—from the East End of his upbringing.

The glitz, the glamour his family would have found showy. Brash. So un-English. So... *American*. And that's what he's grown to love about them, for all their crassness, their loudness, their unerring lack of tact, and style—that they were never afraid to demonstrate what was in their hearts. Even if what was in their hearts was silly, sentimental. And undeserved. And embarrassing. And—perhaps—overdue.

Surely, surely, it will end now?

But no... The standing ovation continues. The wealthy and the well-to-do of Los Angeles.

The angels, indeed, have descended from Heaven tonight.

There are cheers. Cat calls. *Laughter. Nod and a wink to a blind man, Fred, lad!*

He blinks. His eyes are completely dry. He thinks of those who aren't there to clap. The boys who worked in his father's shop, who climbed the ladders, who scrubbed the floor and knotted their aprons in the small of their backs. Who never had less than a good joke for him or a friendly wink. He'd just moved up to a bigger shop, that's all. A shop that sells dreams and nightmares, and advertises its wares with frocks and jewels and perfectly-coiffured women and immaculately-groomed men. The men we want to be, and the women we want to make love to. Or hurt. Because hurt them we always will, whether we want to or not. Weren't they made perfect for that reason? So that our sins could ruin them? And isn't it *our* sin we get a thrill out of that?

He stares out at them. The woman whose scream accompanied the mummified face as it turned in the chair. The woman whose blood ran black in the shower. The man with the pronounced Adam's apple—nervous of girls but devoted to his dear old Mother. The beefcake who fended off flocks of sparrows with a pillow. Others still that he hadn't worked with—the Jewess who sang ballads and starred in comedies, the Cockney who played a bespectacled spy—the other spy, whom he'd cast to rape the kleptomaniac, whose running and escaping in movie after movie was like a child re-enacting his own Mount Rushmore scene, or the villain's back-projected fall from the Eiffel Tower. Producers, dress designers—ah, gowns by the immortal!—casting agents he'd done battle with or seduced with a naughty pun. Names? So many names... So many lives... So many scenes...

All to pay tribute.

All with tears in their eyes.

Too late.

He is seventy-nine, and feels it.

He would rise from the chair if he could.

As it is, he remains seated at the Table of Honour. A vast Buddha as recognisable as any of the actors whose name he put up in lights. Even in silhouette or a few strokes of an artist's pen, he is unmistakable. A household name. A brand name for terror.

His diminutive wife is seated on his right and an actress synonymous with Saint Joan on his left. He is an old man now, suffering from arthritis and fitted with a pacemaker, but whatever is wrong with his heart it is no effort to think both these people beautiful. He does not understand how either of them tolerated his grotesque presence in their lives. How they can show their appreciation, any of them, when he is a mountainous pig. They must be lying. He must be the butt of an enormous joke. His vision swims from the red wine and champagne. He is obese and almost immobile, long sustained by booze and pills. And, if he sometimes knows little else of what goes on around him, he knows he is dying.

Death. Oh yes.

That, my dear—is *suspense*.

The applause falls quiet and the illustrious guests sit down at their tables.

The CBS cameras are looking at him with their big black lenses.

He speaks with his distinctive, lugubrious aplomb in spite of difficulty with the "idiot" cards held up by a floor manager in the penumbra of his vision.

"I thank the AFI for this..." Pause. "'Life *Amusement* Award'..."

Laughter. A Beautiful Blonde in sparkling earrings and immaculate lipstick giggles as she lolls. A passing waiter tops up her glass with bubbly and moves on.

"I believe a man needs three things from sustenance in life," says Fred—now called Fred no longer. "Encouragement, love, and delicious food. All of which have been provided tonight in abundance." A ripple of general thanksgiving. "I also wish to thank my wife for sticking with me through thick and thin. Well, *thick* anyway."

Guffaws and giggles. An actor, Californian teeth, laughs too, leaning over to light the Beautiful Blonde's cigarette.

Her red lips part slightly.

She blows smoke which hangs and drifts.

"And so many of my friends and colleagues..." The old man gazes at the assembled. "...what have I done to deserve this?"

They like that. Another smattering of applause. Faces enraptured. Full of merriment with a dash of the maudlin. A sense of loss, not for what is gone but for something that will not last forever.

"You know, you may think because I make terrifying movies I don't fear very much. But I do. I fear *everything*. "

Eyes and jewels glisten. Silk gowns and black bow ties in the dark.

"For instance, I have a lifelong fear of policemen."

They treat it as a joke—and perhaps it is one. Or has become one through repetition. In the shadows are empty plates, half-full glasses, but no talk. He has their rapt attention. He commands the set.

"When I was a child... I think I was six or seven. Or was it nine or ten?... My father took me to the local police station, and got the sergeant to lock me in a cell for a few hours. I was terrified. When he came back he said: 'Now you know what happens to naughty little boys.'"

Laughter cracks open the reverential silence.

"Now I *do* know what happens to naughty little boys," he says.

This.

Obediently reacting to their cue, once more the audience rise to their feet as he is handed his award by the esteemed director of the AFI, no mean film-maker himself.

Saint Joan embraces him, smooth bare arms stretching around his giant frame. So do his wife and daughter. The warmth of their affection punishes him and makes him feel even more alone, more of a fake. Everyone in the room is genuine, he knows. He is the only actor. The tall man who ran through the crop field attacked by a glider wraps him in a hug. A *real* man. He holds him to his heart. But nobody has come close to his heart. Not really. And it does not even make him sad any more. He would have liked to be tender, but it was never in his make-up. He could be a fool. He could tell a joke, preferably a bad one. Above all he could terrify. He was good at it.

He was a father, he was a husband. But terrifying people was what he did best.

At times, he thought, he'd terrified the whole world.

Flash bulbs are popping.

The old man looks out over his audience of movie-making alumni with no sign of obvious happiness, or any emotion at all—perhaps only half-seeing, half knowing, half believing the adulation. The approval.

The love.

Afterword

Stephen Gallagher

Way back, even if you were indifferent to the workings of cinema, you knew Alfred Hitchcock. With the possible exception of Cecil B DeMille, for decades he would be the only director that an average picturegoer could name. Chaplin and Keaton were comedians, Griffith quickly forgotten, John Ford a studio journeyman. The auteur theory was as yet unborn. But like a DeMille spectacular, a Hitchcock picture was a brand. And like every brand, it came with a defining image.

If you believe the biographers, Hitchcock was sensitive about his ungainly appearance. Yet he exploited it to the full—ruthlessly, you might say. In his signature dark blue suit and tie, he put himself in trailers, in TV spots, on posters. His recognisable silhouette graced a book series, a weekly TV show. Have you seen that unflattering minimalist chubby-faced sketch into which his shadow moved, beginning the opening credits of *Alfred Hitchcock Presents*? That was by his own hand (it was through art skills that he got his first break into motion pictures, designing intertitle cards for the silents).

The show put him into my consciousness long before I saw a Hitchcock film. Like the ghost-edited anthologies that also bore his name and image, the TV stories were twisted tales with a common thread of darkness. Though he only directed a handful out of the hundreds of episodes, the production company was his own and he put his mark on every one. His on-screen introductions and epilogues conveyed the persona of that entertaining childless uncle you once had, a straight-faced humourist, a master of the light macabre. The humour was morbid but it was Charles-Addams morbid, essentially safe, perfectly mirrored in Gounod's solemn and witty *Funeral March of a Marionette* which served as the show's theme.

He was one of the first of our 'household names'. Yet I don't believe we were seeing the real Alfred Hitchcock at all.

I do think I glimpsed him once. The person behind the persona, I mean. There's a short clip from the set of *Blackmail* (1929) which served as a voice test for Polish-Czech actress Anny Ondra. It was never meant for public consumption. Hitchcock appears with her on camera, feeding her lines, winding her up, making her shriek with laughter and hide her face as he ditches the improvised script and accuses her of 'sleeping with men'.

(Ondra comes out of it rather well, but she'd been cast in a silent picture to which the production company had decided to add sound sequences. Rather than work around her accent, they'd go on to shoot the dialogue scenes with her live lip-synching to lines from an offscreen Joan Barry. Does it work? Let's just call it brave. The silent version did better business.)

There's a moment in the clip as the camera starts to roll. It's fleeting, but it's there. Perhaps it's my imagination, but for just a few frames I sense that I'm looking at the real man before the mask goes on.

The hard part lies in defining what I think I see. Let me try to explain. In an old Nativity video from my daughter's schooldays there's a boy, slightly bigger than the rest, who stands there in his hedgehog costume squarely in the middle of the shepherds and the robins. He never sings, never joins in, never reacts to anything onstage, never changes his expression at all. He just looks out into the audience all the way through, a chubby moon face with eyes like little dark buttons. It's as if we're here for his entertainment, not the other way around.

As the jumpy VHS runs and the show unfolds around him, his stillness grows increasingly conspicuous. In family lore his nickname is 'future serial killer'. Though as far as I'm aware, he hasn't lived up to it. Yet.

What do I see in those few frames of the Ondra voice test? Perhaps I imagine it. But I believe I see something like that look.

The taunting of Ondra that follows could be seen as impish, but it's quite possible that if Hitchcock wasn't the director, if it wasn't his set, then he wouldn't be getting away with any of this. While looking online to revisit the clip I came across a *Blackmail* outtake, featured in Matthew Sweet's excellent *Shepperton Babylon* documentary, in which 'Hitch' sneaks into a scene while the camera's running and disrupts it by hoisting up Ondra's dress to look at her underwear.

Again, it's a tease. Show folk are not known for their aversion to mischief and daring. But again, you sense an edge. He's taking advantage. Because he can.

Despite the well-documented pranks on and off the set, and despite Hitchcock's inarguable and lifelong fascination with cool blondes in distress, I don't go the full Spoto on this. By which I mean, I don't think a complex personality can be solved by pointing at its darker traits and shouting 'monster'. Donald Spoto is a celebrity biographer who wrote a 'dark side of genius' study that gave its subject no quarter at all, a portrait of a psychopath driven by sexual obsession with no redeeming features. The biography was a bestseller, and its author would return to the well for at least two further books.

The downside of Spoto's form of 'enlightenment' is that it effectively takes the films away from you. You're left feeling that Hitchcock was a bad man, and appreciation of his art makes you a bad person. You liked those films? Look how wrong you were.

Dare I say it, but I think that in *Leytonstone* we have a more effective psychological key to both the artist and the art.

Hitchcock claimed to be afraid of everything. He saw it as the secret of his success. The story of young Fred's jail cell experience is one that he told often; it appears at the beginning of the famous series of interviews that he gave to French critic and filmmaker François Truffaut. It was his suggested explanation for a lifelong apprehension of police and authority. I've heard the story many times, but can't say I ever felt its impact until I lived through it in this dramatised and extended form.

It's impossible to read these pages without a growing sense of outrage at the cruelty and injustice involved, while feeling the child's lack of any power to resist or even make sense of his plight. This is what stories are for. To feel, as well as to know. Only then can we really begin to understand. You come out of the incident with a head full of scenarios for retribution, for revenge on the police sergeant, with a yearning for some earned repercussion that will punish the father for his act. In Fred's place, you think, I would surely have something to say. I wouldn't take such treatment lying down. I'd make them sorry.

And yet.

He's six years old. While showing us what a profoundly distressing experience this would be, Stephen Volk slots it into the context of the boy's world. Yes, locking Fred into a police cell is a harsh act that's incomprehensible to a child. Yes, these parents are shown to be flawed in their different ways. Yes, authority is inexplicably unjust.

But small children's lives are filled with punishments that seem unfair, in situations they can't understand. So much of life at six years old is spent learning to avoid or appease the anger of adults. Childhood is a rough sea, where the waves don't stop to listen.

Fred was handed over to be 'taught a lesson', though in later life he could never remember what he was supposed to have done to deserve it. So often the lesson that's absorbed is not the lesson that was intended. And the child's priority is not so much to appeal or seek redress, as to work out how to prevent a recurrence without unwittingly making things worse. Usually that means, shut up and keep your head down. Meanwhile the misery will settle. Perhaps it will be dealt with; perhaps it will seep out somewhere else.

It's clear that Fred's imprisonment of Olga Butterworth in an empty house is an act that both springs from his own prison cell experience and prefigures his life's work, which will involve a career spent inflicting psychological distress in the name of art. Fred doesn't want Olga to be hurt, but he does want her to be scared. He feels no conscience at her suffering, and no compunction when he later sees all blame turning onto the victim. It actually gives him pleasure. This is shocking to the reader and while we may continue to sympathise, we like him less and less. It's not even as if Olga had rejected him; this is what she gets for her kindness.

He's found his mojo. Olga is, in effect, the first Hitchcock female lead. She plays in his fantasies, long before he can begin to put those fantasies on celluloid. It's true that Hitchcock had a 'thing' about ice-maiden blondes. He explained it to Truffaut thus: "You know why I favour sophisticated blondes in my films? We're after the drawing-room type, the real ladies, who become whores once they're in the bedroom."

But somehow that doesn't quite cover it. His obsession seemed to be more with the underlying archetype than the individual. It could lead him to cast mediocre talents just because they had the right bones, often to be outshone on the screen by their supporting actresses. For every Madeleine Carroll or Grace Kelly there was a Kim Novak or a Tippi Hedren.

Hedren's testimony provides most of the material for the 'monster' angle on Hitchcock. She considered herself ill-used by the director. First cast in *The Birds*, she was called on again when Kelly backed out of his next project. Hitchcock had acquired the rights to *Marnie*, a novel by British author Winston Graham (also known for his Cornwall-set *Poldark* series). It's about the unravelling of a chameleon-like thief trapped into marriage by a man who's fascinated by her. But something feels broken, here. In Hitchcock's hands, the *Marnie* story became one of cod psychology and perverse sexuality.

Second-time writer-for-hire Evan Hunter reported that the scripting went pretty much to plan until they reached the marital rape scene that takes place on the wedding night of Marnie and Mark Rutland. It's there in the novel, where it's well handled. But Hunter was troubled by the sequence dictated in detail by Hitchcock, which was graphic and brutal. He argued against it, and found himself replaced by Jay Presson Allen. She told him, "You got bothered by the scene that was his reason for making the movie. You just wrote your ticket back to New York."

However, it wasn't the subject matter that caused Hedren a problem.

As she tells it, Hitchcock's response to a personal rejection was to take professional revenge, firstly in the form of sadistic treatment on the set of *The Birds*, and later by sitting on her contract to block offers of A-list projects. Though she was clearly cast above her weight in both of her roles, she believes that Hitchcock ruined her career.

On the rejection claim, I can say nothing. I wasn't there. We've evidence that the younger Hitchcock was known for his horseplay, and one man's horseplay is many a woman's tolerated harassment. I can believe that somewhere inside the dapper English gentleman lurked a creep in a cage. It would explain so much.

But, professionally? Many of the stories that have been used to depict him as a monster—using freezing water to make Janet Leigh scream in the *Psycho* shower sequence, forcing Kim Novak to multiple takes of a plunge into a studio tank for his own pleasure, endangering Hedren with real broken glass to achieve a shot—have been refuted by those actually involved. Some stories only persist because Hitch himself saw the publicity value in encouraging them. On *The 39 Steps*, was it a mean prank to 'lose' the handcuff key and leave Madeleine Carroll shackled to Robert Donat for several hours on their first day of working together? Or was it, as Donat himself believed, a clever move to create the rapport that was directly responsible for their subsequent onscreen chemistry?

Let's have some perspective, here. No one on a Hitchcock production was ever drowned, burned to death, blinded, decapitated by a helicopter, or run down by a train while shooting without a permit. He never raped an underage teen in a Jacuzzi. He didn't cripple horses or bully young women into simulating hardcore lesbian sex. The strongest drug on a Hitchcock set was a glass of champagne at the end of a shoot.

In the modern parlance, Hitchcock certainly had issues. But they were in his head, where they belonged, and where he could make good use of them. Take out the yearning, the fantasy, and the unreasonable obsession from a film like *Vertigo* and you're left with the husk of a story that neither compels nor makes much sense. While with them, you have haunting magic.

(I've a director friend who puts on the *Vertigo* DVD when he's working at home. Not to watch, because he knows the film inside out—he uses it like background music. For ambience, for tone, and as a reminder always to be stretching for something that's just out of reach.)

Leytonstone is about the roots of that genius, the source of those issues. If you don't care to see them, don't lift the rock. But without them a Hitchcock film would be an empty puzzle box, the most common clay of genre unanimated by any spark. Stephen Volk's first-rate novella shows its subject both at the beginning of his life and at its end, still grappling with the duality of love and punishment.

A life built on the stuff of fear and horror, subverted by artifice into something that can speak to us all.

Everyone's story has to begin somewhere. Alfred Hitchcock's began in Leytonstone.

Acknowledgements

I first explored the idea for this novella—sparked by Hitchcock's oft-repeated anecdote about his childhood incarceration—in my short story "Little H", published in *Dark Corners* (Gray Friar Press, 2006). To my surprise, the matter didn't end there. Over several years I began to be intrigued, then fascinated, by the notion that it was merely a jumping-off point. I didn't know whether it was the first act or final act of some larger drama, but somehow I felt in my bones there was far more to explore.

I must emphasise, however, that *Leytonstone* is a work of fiction. (In fact, readers with a passing knowledge of the director's life will notice several glaring inaccuracies: not least the absence of his siblings.) For those seeking, therefore, a thorough portrait of the real film-maker and his films I would recommend Patrick McGilligan's *Alfred Hitchcock: A Life in Darkness of Light*, which far from glossing over his 'dark side' rather puts such accusations in the context of the man and his long and extraordinary career. Amongst countless other valuable sources of insight I'd also flag up (unsurprisingly) the classic *Hitchcock* interviews by Truffaut and, as a primer, the recent BFI compendium *39 Steps to the Genius of Hitchcock*.

In addition I must cite the inspiration of Dr Lenore Terr's articles "Terror Writing by the Formerly Terrified" and "Childhood Trauma and the Creative Product" as well as her book *Too Scared to Cry: Psychic Trauma in Childhood* (1990)—to my mind, essential reading for anyone interested in terror and its consequences.

My thanks must extend to Simon Marshall-Jones for bringing this book to fruition; to Ben Baldwin for his excellent cover; to Stephen Gallagher for his superb Afterword; and to Johnny Mains and Mark Morris, who both gave priceless words of encouragement when they were sorely needed.

Last but not least, I am also deeply indebted to my good friend Chris Smith for his encyclopaedic knowledge of a subject very close to Alfred Hitchcock's heart... Potatoes.

Stephen Volk
Bradford on Avon
January 2015
www.stephenvolk.net

Lightning Source UK Ltd.
Milton Keynes UK
UKOW06f1329270715

255880UK00013B/281/P